CREATURE COMMITTEE

NORM HENDRICKS

SEVERED PRESS
HOBART TASMANIA

CREATURE COMMITTEE

Copyright © 2021 Norm Hendricks

WWW.SEVEREDPRESS.COM

All rights reserved. No part of this book may be reproduced or transmitted in any form or by any electronic or mechanical means, including photocopying, recording or by any information and retrieval system, without the written permission of the publisher and author, except where permitted by law.
This novel is a work of fiction. Names, characters, places and incidents are the product of the author's imagination, or are used fictitiously. Any resemblance to actual events, locales or persons, living or dead, is purely coincidental.

ISBN: 978-1-922551-91-7

All rights reserved.

PROLOGUE

After the failure at Taepodong, the North became extra secretive—even by their standards—about nuclear weapons testing. Whatever the global, political goals had been for the DPRK pulling out of the NPT nuclear treaty, the pressure on the military scientists to produce a working weapon was ponderous. Yoo Se Kwon felt sure this dynamic drove those in charge of Operation Red Star to scale back away from missiles (after two failed launches) and revert to underground testing. They had executed successful subterranean explosions before. Kwon knew the program needed a win, even if a bit retrograde. It's what led Kwon, a onetime doctoral candidate studying the tectonic activity in the South, to infiltrate Red Star. He was afraid of what the testing might bring, and it wasn't earthquakes.

Three…two…one…

It was the third week of testing, each device detonated in a sealed chamber the size of a Brazilian zinc mine, the kind super dump trucks drive in and out of with room to spare. Each device tested was successively more powerful than the previous bomb. The detonation of the third device, this day's test, was said to be the most powerful underground explosion ever detonated. If nothing else, Kwon reasoned, the legend surrounding the sheer mega-tonnage of this bomb might ripple out to the West, commanding respect from the North's great enemy, America.

Kwon studied in America. He was not North Korean. But he did have an enemy, and it too, like an American spy, might take interest in the tests.

"Well, the roof didn't cave in," said a tech from his station of dials. "I suppose that is a success."

"The day is still young," Kwon returned.

The tech, a good natured fellow whose name Kwon could not remember, took the opportunity to tease the seismologist over the usual subject. "What?" he asked, his face contorting with confusion. "I can't understand that strange accent of yours. It's a wonder they allowed you on this project. America rubbed off on you."

Kwon smiled back. "I'm the one who keeps the roof from caving in," he said. "Besides, the military is just as happy to have someone report to the outside world. There are no nuclear secrets to steal, just big firecrackers. If this provokes more tough rhetoric from the West, then our endeavors here are a success."

All totally sensible, except when Kwon went to the observational theater and looked down into the staging area outside the detonation chamber (a chamber also of enormous dimensions where the bombs went off) he saw something that defied sense. Far below, under the crisp glare of stadium lighting, small figures moved about in protective suits, waiting to greet the small platoon of drones coming back from the detonation chamber full of readings and video of the big event.

One of the drones had something stuck in its wheel track, the unmanned vehicle bearing some resemblance to a small tank. Kwon bolted back to the lesser control room he had been relegated to and scanned the bank of screens attached to the numerous cameras mounted in the staging area. He had no control over these cameras so it was difficult to focus on the object the drone had dragged out of the detonation chamber. He scrambled from one monitor to the next, each one offering a teasingly useless view of the odd thing.

That's when the first strike came.

The detonation had been like the others. Though this day's bomb registered higher on the sensors, it felt the same within the auxiliary control room, a low rumble stretching on for such a duration the rocks themselves seemed to be complaining. This impact was different.

The outburst thrust violently through the staging area, causing the techs in the safety gear to flinch. The second impact drove some of them to flee behind the thin safety of the drone vehicles.

The drones had entered the staging area through a small hatch in the larger partition of specially treated steel. It was that wall that had been assaulted by something shaking the metal threshold, loosening rock from the massive granite bed hosting the thick metal divider.

Kwon gaped at the screen that offered the best vantage of the events unfolding below.

Bam!

Another great blow to the metal wall had all the techs scrambling. Yoo Se Kwon ran back out to the observation deck.

"It's happening," he said.

"What is?" his partner asked.

There was no way of saying it. These tests were along the tectonic plate where the failed film shoot occurred all those years ago; where Kwon first met the beast, the creature that had, no doubt, just announced its intention to end the weapon tests upsetting its slumber.

Crack!

A large chunk of granite dropped from the cavern ceiling to land on a drone vehicle, crushing it. By the time the SUV-sized rock rolled away, the drone techs had fled to the airlock.

Kwon had worked the border near this region for weeks, letting out that he was a seismologist in desperate need of work, having firsthand knowledge of how the North sometimes acquired capitalist talent when in need. Operatives grabbed him in his humble accommodations and had him at the testing site in hours. They said he'd get paid for his scientific contributions, but he was not here for work. There was a job here for Kwon, an unfinished one from years ago, one that haunted his dreams. Now, through no fault of his own, others would share the nightmare.

The next strike knocked another layer of granite loose, crumbling down onto the wide staging area.

Kwon eyed the area appearing to take the brunt of the creature's ire.

Not the man-made dividing wall, the one keeping them all safe from the radiation cloud building behind it. The blows seemed focused on areas of rock surrounding the metal wall, but much higher than made sense to Kwon. The thing he had encountered had been a zoological giant, the size of a bull

African elephant but slim and reptilian. How could it reach so high?

Just as the largest wedge of granite crumbled from the manually enlarged cave wall--slipping down into the intermittent glare of the stadium lights--Kwon felt his breakfast dive toward his lower bowel in tandem with the rock's plummet to the staging area.

Something was wrong. It was all wrong, but not in the way Kwon's history with the thing suggested.

We know nothing about this thing's metabolism...

His own words from years ago came back to haunt him. What would happen to this thing when doused with a tsunami of free radicals, a torrent of highly charged ions?

When the rock caging the atomic explosion truly started to fail, the first limb of the creature introduced itself. Then Kwon understood. The clawed foot was every bit the angry crocodilian appendage he had observed on the long ago movie set that had used the creature as a special effects secret ingredient, but now the claw was the size of a Fiat.

An almost oddly comic moment happened as the next thrust by the monster shook loose a wedge of granite, sharp as an axe blade, to fall on its own limb, the leg that had asserted itself into the staging area. An angry howl followed the accident, shaking Kwon's innards.

This was the opportunity Kwon had hoped for when he allowed himself to be forced into labor for the North. The size of the monster made no difference. It was a detail that had nothing to do with the geology professor's loose plan. He fled the auxiliary control room for the passageway leading down to the staging area.

The unnamed partner that had been issued Kwon called down after him. "Where…?"

He did not slow.

A labyrinth of steps curled in on itself, the passageway having been drilled out the living rock. The way was narrow and dark, dimly lit by intermittent bulbs strung on a single wire and bolted into the ceiling. Kwon scrambled, almost falling down the rock steps. Everything in the narrow arteriole was a little damp. When he got toward the bottom where the passage of slippery, damp rocks approached the event floor, the dark corridor started to clog with fleeing workers adorned in red, all-covering protective suits. The walls rumbled, but Kwon had a hunch about the material clinging to one of the drones.

At the big hatch opening onto the staging area, the last of the workers pushed past the geologist for the big elevators leading to the surface. Some great calamity occurred beyond the hatch that narrowed to an opening the size of an American football player. Kwon thought he saw more rock crashing around the drones as the stadium lights sputtered. One worker had stayed to attempt to swing the massive steel hatch door closed on the unfolding disaster. Kwon grabbed the man and, not sure if he could hear through the protective gear, shouted and gestured that he would take the worker's place and close the door. The worker surveyed Kwon with wide eyes, hesitated at Kwon's lack of protective outerwear, but then gave Kwon an appreciative tap on the shoulder, fleeing up the passageway.

Kwon did not close the thick door; instead, he swung past it onto the wide staging area.

There was no hesitation. He had this fight with himself already. He could not say which side won, but doubt was gone. He had lost his life as a scientist. When he had returned from his first conscription north of the 38th parallel, he had foolishly thought his colleagues would have been anxious to follow up on what was the greatest zoological find of the last two centuries. He needed their help to prove *it* had happened. More importantly, the thing haunted his dreams. The creature had become his life. Or, rather, had stolen his life. Kwon needed to prove the monster was real, not only so he could once again join the ranks of the respected, but stop it from doing greater harm.

There could be no hesitation, no matter the recklessness of his actions. He had to move forward. Kwon had to balance accounts with the creature, even close them. The only time he was given pause was when he entered the vast staging floor.

Across the flat, polished bottom of what was designed to be a safe space, a foot, like a huge, crocodilian claw, intruded out of the crumbling protective wall, and planted itself on the polished rock floor.

Kwon rounded the bumper of the drone vehicle that had dragged the object out of the test chamber.

Once a rational man, prideful in his own cool temperament (a quality that had cost him an engagement to a fine woman of respectable education), Yoo Se Kwon gave himself over to manic recklessness. A hundred yards from the monstrous appendage that burst the protective wall and allowed a dose of dangerous radiation into the protected zone, the professor focused on recovering the object stuck to the back bumper of the remote control mini tractor.

A growl that might be the abrasion of hundreds of miles of competing tectonic plates or the mating call of a hundred bull alligators, burrowed up out of every inch of the surrounding rock.

Kwon reached for the object. Run through with the smallest of creases, separating what appeared to be rows of gangrenous scales, the thing was just inches away from his grasp. *Just a nub*, he told himself. Like the tip of the tail or something. Allowing a meager hint of hesitation into his actions, Kwon glanced about the small vehicle, discovering a slim storage compartment bolted to the flank. He found a pair of protective gloves there.

He grabbed the object as the remainder of the breached wall—a natural divider meant to contain the bi-products of the underground blast--let loose another monstrous drumstick, a huge column of taloned mass that joined the first leg of the creature and brought down another dump truck's worth of rock onto the polished floor of the chamber. The closest drone vehicle flattened, smashed two dimensional by the rockslide. The head of the thing, still struggling with the aperture it had opened (some sixty-feet above Kwon), was not yet visible, and Kwon thought it never would be, under the ground at least. The whole test site was about to collapse into itself, and then the thing would be free, but now much larger than when Kwon had first encountered it. Some mix of ancient rage and gamma particles had turned the beast into a walking high rise.

He wouldn't be around to see it escape. With the safety gloves on, he grabbed up the hunk of greenish meat, a manageable bit of monster flesh, and, removing his thick, corduroy jacket—as outfitted by the military to workers on the operation—wrapped up the fleshy mass about the size of a small dog and headed for the exit. And, in doing so, would have the monster on his ass. It would do anything to re-acquire this lost nub the geologist had just stolen. This had been Kwon's hope, if not outright plan.

Yoo Se Kwon offered the North a strange asset, any easy catch along the border and one who would re-up, serve one nuclear test site after the other if necessary. In his search for the beast, he committed to the long haul. It turned out not to be necessary. Kwon knew why. It had been the father, Kim Jun Il, who had stumbled across the creature, woke it up. Kwon had been a part of the committee that had contained the beast, put it back to bed. There was no doubt of its slumbering resentment as it lay within the living rock of the North. The son, Kim Jun Un, had, unknowingly, poked the sleeping dragon awake.

Kwon fought his way to the surface, stumbling past his fellow workers into the moonless night. Ducking his head and tilting his hardhat a bit, he made it onto one of the emergency buses ferrying workers out of the zone. The tectonic screams of the beast followed Kwon onto the bus. The normally well-trained, if not docile, soldiers fled alongside the already full buses, some trying to clamber aboard, others dashing for the back of trucks of all kinds heading out into the black. The soldiers yelled and cursed at one another, but Kwon did not pay much attention until he heard a familiar word, a name.

Bulgasari.

The bus floor beneath Kwon's feet shook as another angry cry rolled through the ground, but something occurred to him then.

Even as the secret facility continued to vent terrified workers and despondent soldiers, even as the bit of monster squirmed in his grasp and leaked some sort of vital fluid, Kwon knew he had achieved his essential goal. Years ago, when he had first met the monster, when he had been a younger man, a scientist who had all his rationality overwhelmed and defeated, he helped other humans achieve containment and called it a victory, foolishly believing he could go back to his world of publish-or-perish, the constant reproving of his doctoral thesis.

He knew better now, oh yes. What can one gain from life shattering trauma if not something akin to wisdom? To learn from past errors and make smarter mistakes.

The creature lived in the rock, was the rock, was the land itself. He had come to believe these things.

Outside, behind the evac bus, the ground shook and cracked open, billowing stony detritus. Shockwaves made the bus convulse and Kwon's innards quiver. The ground collapsed down into the testing cavern. The thing screamed and, maybe, the other workers on the bus with Kwon who may have caught a glimpse of the thing the test bomb had awoken told themselves that the collapse was the end of it. Whatever that thing was, it was now crushed under a thousand tons of rock.

The Bulgasari was the rock. This was Kwon's secret. Once he came into understanding of this truth, he had understood that the North's insistence in continuing their verboten nuclear program had further angered the monster.

The Il regime must have their place on the world stage no matter the cost. Kwon almost felt bad for them. No matter the stories that came out of that fated movie production all those years ago, no one could cast blame for embracing disbelief.

There are many landmarks on the Pathway to Heaven. Tenet nine instructs the pilgrim to transform disbelief, to flip it, transmute doubt into openness to endless possibility that offers the infinite to shift the impossible to the possible, the long shot to the likely. And then some things come along that confirm the eventuality of the unthinkable.

Once, he had been a scientist and that had meant a personal vision limited to the quantifiable. Then along came the Bulgasari and Kwon's horizons shifted.

But then Kwon had to recon with the fact that the North would persist with the weapons program even if the monster knocked on their front door. And, now, that's what it was going to do because it *was* the land, and the regime came knocking at its door with mushroom cloud shaped fists.

A puddle of ichor that was likely radioactive enough to ensure the death of everyone on the bus gathered in Kwon's lap, dripping down between his legs and soaking the crotch of his work coveralls. This was a source of satisfaction for Kwon.

Just so long as the Il's kept exploding super bombs underground, the creature would not sleep, and no amount of rock would keep it from striking out, particularly since it was the rock.

But Kwon was headed to where the thing would have to face him in very different conditions. There was a boat.

Once upon a time, Yoo Se Kwon had become close to a smuggler, a man now passed but who had friends and associates that owed him. Kwon had cashed in on these debts and had a boat waiting some fifty miles to the southwest, waiting to launch out into the Yellow Sea. If the monster wanted this chunk of itself back—Kwon knew it would—the thing would have to prove its worth on the water.

He would have to find some better shielding to wrap around the monster bit. He wanted to be able to choose his battleground. The chief ingredient, the last tile in the mosaic plan to reenter the North and confront the Bulgasari lay in his ability to counteract dangerous levels of radiation he was now absorbing.

Six months ago, Kwon had happened upon some research done by the CIA in response to Russian intelligence network's love for polonium poisoning. Strangely enough it would become a bit of a lesson in art history, where people got the materials for the first pigments we now take for granted and some unusual properties of minerals involved in creating a particular color deep within the blue part of the spectrum.

The fissure widened around them. Another bus just outside the windows to Kwon's left fell to its side as the ground fled from the tires on its right flank. In a second more the bus was gone, the screaming of the workers inside mixing with the angry cries of the earth itself and its vicious defender.

The monster was coming.

ONE

What am I to say about my friend, Yoo Se Kwon? First, we came to call him Yuz--as in OG gangster talk: Hey, youz guys. Yuz came to us as a gift of the Yellow Sea, while we were sailing as operational support for South Korean naval training exercises, the ones meant to piss off the North Koreans. There he came, bobbing up to us on relatively calm seas, barely holding onto an empty chlorination tank from the sewage processing system typical to a destroyer class ship. We were not aware of such a ship being lost. The scuttling of a destroyer would have produced a major alert, with possible rescue operations ensuing. Of course, you could never tell with the North. They kept to themselves.

We were on the *Merrymount*, a general purpose, explorer class vessel, and she was a good ship. When we pulled Yuz out of the drink we were running about twelve nautical miles outside of Incheon. That's the distance a vessel must be from shore to dump untreated waste into the sea. We were ensuring the Yellow Sea stayed yellow. Normally, something as small as a single survivor would be a long-shot discovery, even for a relatively small vessel like ours (ninety feet from perpendicular to perpendicular), but we had cut engines, just floating out there, already searching the waters because of some strange stuff being picked up on SONAR.

Could have been related to the scuttling of the ship, we may have made that connection in later reflection. If there had been a later.

"Hey, Iceman!" a voice called to me as I took charge of the gurney sporting our newly arrived guest. I can easily say, ol' Yuz was in bad shape. The Iceman would get him below deck.

"They call me Iceman because I'm as cool as they come," I said to Yuz's still form. I thought I saw a little life. Not much, but I thought he should know: I'm the Iceman.

"Bean," the Quartermaster yelled after me. "When you get that piece of flotsam stowed, officers' mess needs another load of ice." The petty officer next to him giggled.

They also call me Bean. That one is because my full name is Ensign Gary Pinto, direct from Cherry Hill, New Jersey.

"No time," I said. "We got ASD at thirteen."

"Abandon ship drill's been cancelled, Bean-o," he said. "We've got to investigate those hinky SONAR blips."

"More junk islands," I muttered, leading our new friend to the infirmary where Petty Officer Rathman was recovering from self-poisoning by way of downing a container of rubbing alcohol. Rathman had been dealing with the DT's. He had a problem.

The Korean guy I later came to know as Yuz was gripping a bundled hunk of something he had been clutching with the arm that wasn't locked onto the empty chlorinator tank. He dropped it as they bumped him up over a hatchway. I ignored the quartermaster's squabble about refitting the brass with ice for the cocktail hour. I followed the gurney and the corpsman who had taken Yuz the last few steps into the infirmary. I grabbed ahold of a dangling saline bag, so they let me stay.

When they got the, as yet unknown, soaking Korean onto a bed next to the sad looking Rathman, I secured the ragged, also wet, bundle in the floor locker next to the bed. As the patch of rough covering material I took for burlap flapped open, I got a brief glance at the elongated section of something that had been clearly sawn off something much larger. Something with scales.

Odd, heck yeah, but it all got weirder because as I was stowing the thing--clearly none of my business—a flap on the opposite side kicked open. The impression I received of a lizard tail was gone, and in its place was what could only be described as a hunk of garbage…wet garbage. A plastic grocery bag released a fistful of seawater before I closed it up and got it stowed. I ignored the puddle on the floor and got the heck outta Dodge before someone made my mess my problem.

I looked to skedaddle and get to the mindless, safe duties a lowly ensign might get heaped upon him on an exploration class ship in the middle of posturing maneuvers in the Yellow Sea.

Not too long after, there was more shit work for a whole Navy's-worth of lowly squids. The odd SONAR blips got explained, along with our guest's package, when a floating island of garbage snuck up on our port. Not our first rodeo, rounding up the numerous garbage islands issuing out of regions south of the 38th parallel. Since China--cousin to the neighbor to the North that shall not be named, and owner of the world's largest recycling plants--refused to process refuse from the peninsula's capitalist pride, the South Koreans, the seas endured the birthing of these islands of bi-product from the imitable manufacturing success of Samsung phones, Kia automobiles, and Gangnam Style jewel cases.

And when I say we were putting some time into this garbage island, I mean it was sort of our loose mission as an explorer class vessel (smaller than a PT boat). We were to log data on anything anomalous and, during commie-annoying exercises, anything was worth measuring. An island made of refuse qualified as worth a weigh-in, according to the captain. Could be God had an opinion on the *Merrymount's* mission, but as the joke goes, God's a bit down the chain of command from the skipper.

This of course meant next-level shit duties, so I went to go check on our guest instead.

I spent the better part of the afternoon stocking the officers' mess. On a larger ship, they'd have an apprentice seaman do this. On a British flagship that might still be a cabin boy, but here in the US Navy we got ensigns like myself.

Cramming myself into the relatively unused infirmary, I was doing a bang up job of avoiding my cabin boy duties as described to me by the captain by way of the petty officer.

I was surprised to find this bit of human ballast conscious, to a degree, and looking about with bleary eyes.

He looked about and said something loopy and Korean.

Anticipating the intent, I jumped over and grabbed the package he had been holding tight while bobbing on the gently rolling waves of the Yellow Sea.

Strangely, he seemed less than happy to see the bundle.

"A cage," he said, his brow crinkling up.

"What?" I asked, holding the bundle so that the blanket covered it completely. "I don't get you, mac. What about a cage?"

“A Faraday cage,” he said, eyes locked on the bundle. “It is best placed in a Faraday cage with a lead top.”

“You speak some good English,” I said. “And yet, I don’t know what you’re talking about.”

Doctor Ormsby (Lieutenant Ormsby) piped in from his computer terminal. “He’s referring to containing the thing in such a way to block magnetic or electric waves. And, no, we don’t have one.”

Outside, thunder rumbled from a position so close it rattled the glass tubes on a stand in the corner of the small room.

“Here comes that storm MAFF promised,” Rathman said from his bed. His eyes remained shut. “MAFF stands for Korean Ministry of agriculture, forestry, and--”

“And we don’t care,” I said, sure Rathman was going directly from his infirmary bed to a facility in Japan to dry out. “Better secure your goods, Doc, this can only mean rough seas. Means we’re gonna give on the garbage island and try to skirt this front. Meanwhile, I’m going to see if I can find the next best thing to day fair cage…”

“Faraday,” Doc corrected. “He was a guy.”

“Yeah, that,” I said and leaned in a bit to our Korean guest. “Now that you’re awake, I’m thinking the skipper might want a word. We’re awfully close to the 38th. They’ll want to know which side you came from.”

“It must be locked up where there is copper surrounding,” he said, “and don’t forget the lead.”

“Most tell me to get the lead out, not in.” I offered a grin.

The Korean looked exhausted, but he managed a smirk in return. “There is an element of urgency, Ensign. Lead out of the pockets, and lead in the shielding, and you’ll be on the righteous path.”

We held our friendly gaze. “I’ll do my best...uh…”

“Yoo Se Kwon.”

“Well, Yoo--”

“Family name,” Doc interrupted.

“I know,” I said. “I just like that part of the name best, more likely to remember it. Mr. Yoo, don’t you worry; I’ll get this locked down tight.”

That's when Yuz locked eyes with me. "Copper," he said. "The correct path involves copper shielding, otherwise it will seek to retrieve."

"It?"

But Yuz said no more. His eyes slid closed, and he was out. There were no discernable cuts or bruises on the man, but no doubt he was as waterlogged as a paper boat in a hurricane.

I went to turn to leave, not noticing someone had come up behind me.

"This him?" the captain asked, directly into my forehead.

Yeah, he was tall; it's not like a prerequisite for the rank, but it sure helped. His high-and-tight cut beneath his cap had plenty of pepper mixed in with the salt. The man had been around: navigated the warm waters of the Persian Gulf like it was a kiddy pool in his backyard. Iraq, both of 'em.

"That's Yoo Se Kwon," the doc said. "His lungs are relatively clean. Just worn out and dehydrated near to death."

"That's not his only problem," Cap said.

Doc swiveled away from his computer monitor. "Oh?" he said. "Brought your magic med specs did you, Don?"

Captain Donald Hanhold didn't care for the crew being informal with him. Doc Ormsby was the exception; he'd seen some Persian Gulf too.

Skipper scoffed. "If you'd check your belt buckle you'd know the problem, Luke."

Doc looked down at the leather belt, a bit of gut spilling over. He looked back at Cap with a puzzled look. Cap pointed to the far left hip where Doc's lab coat had just flapped closed. The doc worked with an old x-ray machine. Standard Naval policy: any personnel working with radiation had to wear a dosimetry indicator badge while on duty. What was normally a white hexagon going largely ignored on his belt, was now an angry red.

"Better wear your lead underwear around our friend here," Cap said. "He's as radioactive as hell."

***

"As your new pal, Gary, pointed out," the cap said across the small table, "your English is very good."

"I studied at Berkeley for a time, geology with a concentration in seismology," Yoo Se Kwon said. "They took me when I was doing field work for my doctoral thesis."

"Who took you?" I asked.

The cap gave me a look with his icy grey eyes that had a harsher tone than I've ever heard him use verbally. "You seem to have hit it off with ensign Pinto here so that's why I've invited him to this interview with the direct caution that he is not to talk."

I shrugged and returned to loading the ice. We were in the officers' mess, as humble as it is aboard an explorer class. I was the Iceman, after all. I tried to be quiet about it.

"Mr. Yoo--"

"Gary has taken to calling me Yuz," the Korean said. "That seems to work."

"Yuz," the skipper continued. "I hope you appreciate my position. I've got an unidentified Korean on my hands shooting out more rads than Oppenheimer's undies. I think you can appreciate my suspicions."

"Yes," Yuz said. "I am coming from North Korea where I had been working at the secret nuclear testing site your government has been trying to discover for some time."

"An underground site?" Captain Hanhold asked. "It would have to be. That would explain why they want someone watching out for earthquakes, I suppose. Don't want the whole shebang going up because of a few ground ripples."

The master-at-arms stood like a cigar store Indian in the corner. Yuz eyed him and then looked at his fingers on the table before responding. He was wrapped up in one of those tinfoil looking blankets, an emergency thermal piece; this one had lead coil sewn into the stuffing to act as emergency containment for fuel rods on a nuclear vessel--now standard issue on all vessels because it was cheap to produce. It kept him warm and us safe from his glowing personality.

"I have not worked as a seismologist since I was brought to the North," Yuz said. "They kidnapped me, again. This time it was my idea."

The captain was silent a bit, running a powerful-looking hand over his forehead, leaving his cap askew. "Well," he said at last, "going to have to keep you under wraps, in a number of ways. We can't have you irradiating the crew, can we?"

"What is emitting from my body can be tolerated. I've taken measures to ensure this," Yuz said. "What of my package? It is an object of great importance, and like myself could be hazardous."

I dropped in the rest of the ice with a clack that made the guard's hand drift up to his sidearm. "Don't worry, Skipper," I said. "I got that bundle of his tucked in nice and snug into an IP-3 box down below."

"An IP-3?" Yuz asked.

Skipper made an odd square shape with his fingers as though to replace the slideshow part of a sales pitch on the *Merrymount*'s radioactive materials containment facilities.

"A solid steel frame with a free-floating inner sheath with bits of lead glass--"

"I know the components of a typical IP-3," Yuz said, clearly worked up. "It is desperately insufficient for our needs."

"Care to let me in on what *our* needs are?" Cap asked.

"Radioactivity is not the chief threat the object poses."

The captain stood with a grunt. He was a tall guy in a tight space, kind of his story aboard his ship. "The thing down below or the low level rads you're putting out?" he asked. "You're hazardous in other ways, my friend. Politically radioactive. I've put a call into PACOM in Aiea. I'd be surprised if the NSA wouldn't want a word with you. We're going to have to process you for--"

"Cap'n."

Ensign Boregard poked in his head, interrupting Yuz's debriefing.

Skipper offered the Korean a thin smile. "You'll have to excuse me," he said.

Yuz nodded. "Actually, if I could return to my bed…"

"You just wait there."

Hanhold followed the ensign into the entryway. I let the cubes fall slower onto the tray for officers' soft drinks so I could hear.

"What is it?" The skipper sounded like he was in no mood.

"It's a case of good news...uh, weird news, cap'n," the ensign, sounding like he was standing on glass barefoot, stammered.

"Let's have it."

"We got around that storm; we're running about fifty M-n-M's outside hey-Jew--"

"JeJu, Ensign."

"Right, Cap," Ensign said. I could almost hear him gulp. "Well, got outta the way of that storm anyway. And, here's the weird part, there's a garbage island sitting right off our aft."

"Another one?" Captain Hanhold asked. "Well, the white coats in Honolulu will want to know about that."

"No, Cap; not another one, the same one."

"What? That's not possible. What is the dog watch drinking?"

"We all saw it, Cap, and we all had a plenty close up look at it before. There are telltale components that would be even more unlikely than running into another pile."

"What the hell are you talking about?"

"You should come look, Cap."

There was a heavy sigh. Hanhold poked his head into the mess. "Bean-O, take your pal here back to his bed while I sort this out."

And *my* Yuz sure was tired, leaning pretty heavily on me all the way back to the infirmary. I didn't know if it was because I found him or what, but I gotta tell you, I liked this Yuz. Toughest thing to get stuck with on a ship the size of the *Merrymount* was a blabbermouth, and, brother, this guy was not it.

"The American Navy keeps dogs on their boats?" he asked as I plopped him down.

"Dog watch, the seamen currently charged with standing watch," I explained. "Though on a boat this size, everyone on deck has to keep a sharp eye. We're a hybrid research vessel, log what we find. Garbage mostly."

"What were they talking about, the garbage island?"

"Yeah, those are all over this area, with all the industry in South Korea and earthquakes in Japan. Well, you should know with your package and all."

"My package?" he asked, pulling up a sheet and starting to drift away. "What about it? I should check on your containment procedures later. It is very important, isolation."

"Well, from what I saw it looks like you've been spending time keeping track of ocean garbage yourself."

His eyes opened. "Me? Garbage? Please explain."

"That's what I saw when I accidentally, and, please, it was an accident, peeked under the cover. I saw ocean garbage."

Yuz shot up straight in bed.

"We must leave here at once."

"The infirmary?"

"No, the ship, all of us. Can you sound an alarm?"

Before I could answer, the alarm for All Hands was already going off.

Yous guys, I said in my best Cagney accent when I was talking to Yuz. *Yuz?* He had asked. You are attempting to speak Korean? I had laughed. *Hah, I didn't think so.* And Mr. Kwon found it funny too. Nicknames stick like peanut butter on a small ship. After all, I am the Iceman.

Hard to figure how he did it, as waterlogged as he was, but my Korean pal--from the North, South, or East of Oz--leapt up from that bed (on this ship even the Doc needs to head up for All Hands) and grabbed me by the upper arm. Some part of me had time to register an opportunity to defend myself. There are any number of wrist bends they trained into me I could have used to release myself from the now crazed Korean's kung fu grip, but I used none of these.

"Where are we going, Yuz?"

He looked around wildly at an empty passageway. Most aboard were more mobile than us and were already on deck. This was evidenced when barked orders from above turned to the first scream.

"We must leave this ship, now," he said. "I tried to keep the lobe away from it. One's first thought, of course, is to establish proof in cases like these."

"Cases like what?" I said, then yanked my arm away. "Look, Yuz, I like you, feel responsible for you, but I am military personnel. I have certain training--"

He had me moving again, the grip on me convincing without being menacing.

"An exceptional sense of humor is essential to survival in the face of the apocalyptic."

"The what?"

"The seventh rule to the path of Heaven, Gary, is an open heart," he said. "Please repeat that back to me."

They had warned me. When things get weird, it's like being flushed down a whirlpool the size of MetLife Stadium where the Giants play. I thought they--any number of RDCs or angry commanders--were trying to prep me for war. I suddenly wished one of them had been named Alice because I had the feeling we were nose-to-nose with the looking glass, about to press our way through.

"Yuz, I--"

Then the alarms changed. The Navy is all about learning a long series of non-verbal codes. That's what comes from having to communicate between floating asylums with the expectation that radios, cell phones, sat-phones, and all other bug-a-boos of the modern world will break down and, at any minute, one will be thrust back to the high seas of the 17th century, fighting off privateers in the name of the Queen.

"This is what must happen," Yuz said. "We must get to the surface, and you must get us to a lifeboat. What should happen is that you should try not to focus on anything you see on deck, but you really should focus on the Path to Heaven.

"Is that your way of telling me you're going to kill me?"

He smirked. "No, my friend," he said, looking about (never consulting me on which way to go). "I am telling you about my belief system. Number seven, the open heart."

And we were off. He shoved me toward a utility tube leading to a deck hatch.

"There are stairs," I pointed out. He was not listening, but the screams compelled me to obey.

We climbed, and as the man first to the hatch, and the one not lost at sea, I was more than pleased to muscle open the hatch and head out into the sun.

Except, there was no sun. We were at the edge of the storm, but even the weak orb reminding us of its presence behind the leaden layer of clouds was obscured by the thing looming over the *Merrymount*.

TWO

Tenet two for those following the Path to Heaven requires contemplation of the unknowable. This is what Yuz told me as we paddled away from the attack on the *USS Merrymount*.

Yes, it was a court martial worthy offense to abandon a ship while under attack, but it was the thing attacking the ship that erased my relationship to protocol or my career.

Who knows when the thing would return the sun to us, a living mountain looming up over the explorer ship as though playing with a bathtub toy.

It's the tires, Cap, the dogwatch had said as all hands took to the deck and the seaman pointed down into the island of junk, still floating along with the ship, bobbing peacefully if not a bit mysteriously. *No junk island we've tracked ever had 'em. They're white, kinda weird, but see them? See how they float along there kinda weird, how they seem to look at you?*

And maybe those weird eyes floating among all the other flotsam winked or blinked because, just before all hell broke loose, the crew gasped and reeled back.

Now the shadow was upon us, and though I followed this man, essentially a stranger, into the water just outside Japan, I felt like I had betrayed my crew for those two eyes--tires rolled off some hellish eighteen-wheeler--turned on them. The captain barked orders I could not quite make out as the engines roared to life. I was being left behind, yet I felt safer for having escaped, for the moment, the attention of the mountain.

It moved and thunder followed from the distant storm we put behind us; or rumbled up from Davy Jones' ocean bottom where one could believe this thing could plant its feet. The looming garbage mountain turned, and I could see then the difference from the multicolored, multi-form junkyard-caught-in-a-cyclone and the reptile hiding behind this facade. I wiped sweat from my eyes, the PFD practically choking me out as I tried to get the motor working for the captain's gig.

I swear I did not know that Yuz had hauled me into it.

The part of the mountain closest to us, the keel of the upended battleship, revealed to me its flip side, its secret bilge beam, its true self. Where the junkyard on the far side of the mountain obscured itself at some obtuse azimuth, the underbelly exposed to us--though as much in the shadow of the mountain as the *Merrymount*'s poop deck--exposed the long, latitudinal belly bands of a reptile. I was reminded of my visions in the infirmary.

Yuz took my elbow. "It moves, and turns its back on us, taking many forms," he said. "But make no mistake. It is the snake that waits in the long grass. It is Hanja, the Bulgasari, bringer of all things, the taker of all things."

There was nothing to say to this, and that jibed because I could not talk but only watch as a section of abandoned refrigerator doors and supermarket bags struck down from somewhere in the middle of the serpentine trash spire and obliterated the ship's focsle, the crew fleeing midship like members of an ant colony just as your little brother steps on it, or a white mouse that just now realized it had been let loose from the pet store box only to land on the newspaper lining of the cage for some kid's boa constrictor.

There were screams. I hate to describe it, thinking back. If it had been war, some bell of pity would buoy up appropriately, but this was something else.

How many times have I been called upon to report on these things? I can only tell you the telling only gets less real, though the story remains the same because the events were what they were.

The reptilian limb came down.

Some more effective version of what we think of as a tyrannosaur's watchmaker's hands, a titanic falcon's claw made of soccer balls and Styrofoam coolers, swept down and bisected the *Merrymount* from forecastle to poop deck. The screams were an accompaniment to a horror movie carnival ride I had been strapped down into.

As the light played between the edges of the far squall to wash over the back of the beast, the limb that lashed appeared more moving landfill than dragon paw. Metal crumpled like cardboard and the subsonic complaint of the *Merrymount's* steel supports seemed to issue from my guts.

They were in the water then, my shipmates, who did not know why the vengeful beast swatted at them with first its claws then with a tail that was a sausage casing packed with trash. There was blood. The ocean purpled with it. The wake from the action sent a gentle wash runneled with crimson. I drew back, afraid it would land in my mouth, the salt of the sea and the copper salt of my dying crewmates' blood.

Though they looked largely like the exposed ribs of a beach umbrella, the nasty claws flashed out and down, cutting and cutting, abruptly halting the drowning cries.

Someone grabbed my hand, but when I looked down it was I who grabbed blindly for Yuz, glad to have found him. He looked at me with grave concern.

They must have all been dead because it no longer seemed to need the disguise. The umbrella ribs gone, someone I called friend, and more than that, shipmate, dangled, pierced by one of the long, black claws descending from limbs covered in scales the size of garbage can lids.

I think it was the boatswain mate. The body slipped from the claw that began to piece through the wreckage. Loose shouts trailed us, but gouts of smoke from the heart of the torn vessel obscured the scene.

"It will reclaim its own," Yuz said, nodding as the beast pulled away from the smoke cloud, a reptile that could consume all of Spielberg's dinosaurs and the island they live on in one big gulp. On the claw that had skewered my friend, a hunk of reptile meat clung like a booger then disappeared. "Reabsorbed," Yuz explained.

"What just happened?" I asked the ocean.

The creature slowly lowered itself into the slate ocean. The verticals were now horizontals and the gutted diesel found the main engine. The monster head lit up red as flames wriggled through the fists of smoke. Then the creature was gone. The ship sank not long afterward. Yuz got the motor running about the time the captain's head knocked up against the bow of the little boat we had taken from him.

There are many landmarks on the road to Heaven. Tenet five requires angelic forgiveness. The followers of the road must write down their grievances on a slip of rice paper, then release them into the firepit so that the ashes may fly up to Heaven to prepare the way of the true believer.

"Why are you telling me this?" I snapped at Yuz.

The motor had cut out long ago.

He looked far away to the horizon, not answering me, sitting there quietly until his gaze forced me to check the calm seas, check it for garbage, check it for a lizard tail the size of a freight train. We were adrift. Yuz appeared adrift too.

"How does one do it?" he asked, slowing turning toward me. "How does one make sense of what just happened to your ship, to your shipmates, to you?"

"What *did* happen to us?" I asked, feeling an electric eel swirl in my gut, urging me toward freaking the fuck out. "Huh? Can you tell me that? What?"

Using the thwart as a billet, Yuz settled on the board across the middle as best he could, ignoring my urgency. He appeared to be fine with floating out in the middle of nowhere. And, I suppose, he had reason. He had done it before. At least he was dry and had company this time.

"I'm sorry, Bean," he said, looking up at the sky. "You have been drawn into something from which there may be no escape, not until it ends, if it does."

"What are you even--"

"The thing, the creature," he said. "It is called the Bulgarasi, and it is the product of a secret project gone wrong."

"Nuclear weapons testing?"

"No," he said, "a movie production."

I felt like I was going to vomit. "Maybe we shouldn't spend our last hours on this planet talking," I said. A rumbling of distant thunder caused me to flinch and gaze toward the horizon, a war of crimsons and violets.

Red sky at night, sailor's delight.

"I did not mean to bring harm to you or your associates," he said. "The path tells us that sometimes roads converge towards purposes with no road signs."

"Yeah," I said, curling up in the bow of the craft that was just slightly larger than a dinghy, "I'll take silence over riddles."

But the horizon gave up its color, and the clouds on the outside of the passing squall served up our next unhappy turn by departing. The cold stars cast off any residual warmth from the grey day. I curled up tighter against the dropping temps, hungry and cold. At last, I couldn't take it, desiring escape from thinking about my discomfort.

"A movie?" I asked. "A movie about what? The Bulgarasi?"

I was not too good on my local lingo, but I had picked up on one term. A Chinese term picked up by sailors working the Pacific Theater. Cumshaw, a trade, a bad trade, a trade you get stuck with because there's only bad options ahead.

My eyes adjusted to the moonlight, and I could see Yuz's far-away look, and I knew he was going to unload a galley full of bilge water on me, and I'd have to swallow it. This would be our cumshaw, trade, for distraction from the conditions I felt sure would kill me.

"The Bulgasari," he said at last, "was an ancient creature created by a lowly blacksmith who forged it from the crushed bones of his daughter, slaughtered by the evil king cracking down on local tax evaders. The Bulgasari, a monster noted for its hunger for metal, defeats the armies of the king, devouring the armaments of the evil king's military. But, the king was wily; he kidnapped the younger daughter of the blacksmith, forcing the smith to betray his creation, luring it to a copper mine and burying it alive, trapping it for all time. When the king kills the second daughter, the smith saved the blood from the girl and poured it into the ground where it soaked down into the Earth's core and re-awoke the Bulgasari that emerged from the ground and devoured the king."

I grunted in protest. "Which one were you, the blacksmith? The second daughter?"

"I tell you the legend of the Bulgasari to prepare the path for my story," he said. "I wish that I could say that what happened to me was any less fantastic."

THREE

The Korean Peninsula runs into contact with a geologic feature known as the Pacific Mobile Belt. Strangely, Yoo Se Kwon only learned this once he was at Berkeley where he studied geology and was working on his doctoral thesis. He was performing research for this thesis about ten miles south of the 38th parallel in the Gyeonggi province when they took him. It was the nineties, and it was the era of stewardship of the people's servant, the most noble Kim Jong Il, leader of the Democratic People's Republic of Korea. It was a time not long after the passing of Il's father, Kim Jong Sung, and the new leader was looking to make his mark on the world, spread Korea's particular brand of red philosophy. *Godzilla Versus Space-Godzilla* marked the twenty-first installment of the Japanese franchise, a cinematic release that would prove to be fateful for the new Korean ruler and Yoo Se Kwon.

Yuz and his team of undergrad interns from Seoul National University had set off a series of charges, sounding for pockets of limestone along the Amurian Plate, a tectonic horizon known only for occasional rumblings that sometimes exposed a vein of Uranium. Which is what Yuz thought brought the North Koreans over the border in the first place. He did not know they had been on the wrong side of 38 for weeks, disguised as South Korean regulars in search of unwilling workers for the new leader's secret project. In the most rural areas, the border between the two countries was, in stretches, unrecognizable.

As lost as they were, the unmarked platoon of bugs (short for Korean slang equivalent of grunts--bugjjog) rolled up on the detail of rock measurers in good spirits. For reasons unknown

to this platoon of bugs, their most recent hauls of unwilling workers were big improvements,

health-wise, over their first catch of conscripts. Though they did not know it, having never ventured into the South on purpose, quality of life for South Koreans was significantly better than survivors of the North.

This could be because of the bug-lord's grab-bag of well-conceived policies, including grand military and purposeless infrastructure projects (just see the Bukhan River hydro-electric dam where some comrade forgot to grease the bearings in the turbines so that the whole thing blew apart in the second day after activation) in conjunction with reallocation of petroleum away from artificial fertilizers toward the ginormous new super-max mid-air refueling jet, the M-9--cheap knock off of the Chinese Il-39; Il bought five and maxed out their fuel payload...never used.

Subsequently, strangely, crops all over the rocky-soiled North failed leading to the newest social policy son-of-Sung referred to as Biog Biog, the re-fertilization. Citizens were invited to stop by the local argo field to do their business. When this proved insufficient, untreated solid waste was shipped from three of the largest citizen housing complexes near agricultural centers. Here's the odd statistic, freak-o-nomically speaking, seventy-six percent of the population in these regions turned up with ringworm, hookworm, and roundworm (and several other geometric shapes in the form of worms). And, surprise, none of this wholesale crapping-where-you-eat vega-tology did little to stem the widespread food shortages sweeping the rural districts along the border.

Yuz later learned that this particular Shanghai-ing platoon had been sent to work along the parallel. Yuz and his team began to realize the reasoning behind this inexplicable order that seemingly threatened war for the sake of acquiring labor for a new project. The leadership hoped this labor acquisition team would, accidentally, lay hold of some more able-bodied South

Koreans and waylay them. Since rolling over a shallow section of the Yalu (the dry season coming to an end), the local population (still facelessly rural villages to this merry band) had a lot more spunk. In fact, they had all escaped.

"Can we help you?" Yuz said to the man loping off the transport.

Instead of answering, the man--dressed in a nondescript, rough cut worker's jumpsuit-- stepped forward and whipped

Yuz across the noggin with the .45 he'd slipped from the pocket of his worker blues. When Yuz's grad students gasped, the other men leaped from the transport, pointing guns at the geologists. This group was not going to get away.

"We are grateful you set off charges," the leader said, his bug accent relatively light but easily identifiable. "We have been wandering around this wasteland for days. Thanks to my lieutenant, lost. I had grave doubts as to our ability to complete our mission, but, well, here you are, aren't you? And what healthy specimens you all look like, very rugged indeed. By your sunburns I see you are all used to difficult work in the out of doors. Excellent. Load them up!"

"Professor?" It was Chan Hee; she was only twenty years old. She never came home from the North.

"It will be fine," Yuz told her, not really sure if it was a lie. "We'll help with the potato crop and be back working our research within a week."

Yuz looked at the captain of the communist pirates who shrugged. "Sure," he grunted.

"It is well known," Doyoon said. He was the transfer student from Yonsei. "It is well known about the packs of North Korean soldiers who travel across the parallel to get able bodied workers during harvest. There are too few smuggler ships bringing contraband food across the various blockades to keep the people of the North fed. They need these harvests to survive the winter. Tell yourself it is a humanitarian mission. Conditions are bad for our northern cousins. Imagine being so starved and full of ringworm that your weakness will not allow you to harvest the food that will save you."

Yuz's crew allowed themselves to be loaded into the truck headed for the angry river passage that flowed through a mountain tunnel that the CIA did not know about and South Korean intelligence did not tell them for this very reason: no matter the results of the war of the 1940s, the people of the North were still, on some level, family and sometimes needed the assistance of their more affluent and worldly southern cousins. The students and their professor told themselves it was a humanitarian mission.

Three months later, they were still working in the North on Il's special project. Except,

Chan-hee had died, a victim of the project's subject.

The chairman had said it would be the most powerful form of propaganda ever released onto the world. Yuz knew differently. The old man just loved monster movies.

Strangely, their skills as geologists proved valuable. The ability to use and read a seismograph (as out of date as the Northern device was) helped the director manage the supposed propaganda film's star. The star of this film was a captive too, but could be more temperamental than the greatest diva.

"They found it when they were digging out Old Man there," Cannady said, jerking a thumb at the largest of the local mountains. "They were tunneling to set up an underground military installation. They were gearing up to put in a nuclear test site, when they uncovered the thing. As my granny would say, shag-on-a-gum tree, they plum forgot all about another nuclear test when the thing got up and started walking."

Sean Cannady was an Australian smuggler who stayed in port a little too long and ran into the bad luck of being conscripted into helping make the ultimate propaganda piece, the story that would be seen by the world and bring with it the glorious light of the people. He was strong and skilled, just when both those things were at an absolute premium in the name of creating Il's masterpiece.

Cannady, going by Keekee, was in charge of wrangling the star of the movie out of its accommodations.

"The thing doesn't care for being in the open air," Keekee said, stoking the coals under the forge, "but once we get it to the cave mouth, she'll be good as apples; it will get a whiff of the smoldering steel and come out for the cameras. Run the copper sluice down through their miniature buildings and Sicko's director will have some of the greatest footage ever slapped on celluloid, by right he will. Your crew ready with the light show?"

Yuz nodded. He knew English just fine; it was necessary in advance of his studies at Berkeley. He knew too, Keekee's reference to the Glorious Leader of the People. Il had become Sicko to them.

Yuz, Keekee's right hand, didn't feel much like talking, as he had to watch ten people in his charge--Chan Hee one of them--get attacked during yesterday's failed shoot. Most days were failures, but Il's crew had orders to finish the film and the chancellor insisted on having the film feature at least an hour of high quality footage of the glorious leader's great find, *the creature.*

This monster movie would have an actual monster.

A bullhorn assaulted them from half a soccer field away.

"What's he saying, mate?" Keekee asked.

Yuz translated. The Australian actually spoke passable Korean, but the squawks squirting out of the bullhorn were difficult to confirm as actual words.

Keekee scoffed. "Go time, huh?" he said. "You know this is going to go like all the other days of production, don't 'cha? I mean, they sent the human stars home, didn't they? The chiseled-jawed scientist and his love interest, the young woman army major who just couldn't love a man the way she loved Karl Marx. Haven't even seen the erasable-but-lovable factory worker. It's just us and the real star of this misbegotten production, her lovely majesty herself. Don't look at me like that, it's a female, by-gum. If you had been married as many times as…wait...feel that? What's the seismograph tellin' us, love?"

The graphite on the old model jiggled across the graph scroll with palsied intensity. "We will not need secondary measures to encourage it," Yuz said.

"The dragon," Keekee said. "It's what you want to call it. I hear it in your voice even when you avoid the term, particularly when you avoid the term. You'd just as soon that it go back to the subterranean hell they found it in. 'Cause, as we have learned, if it comes out it won't be to deliver any of the juicier lines from the script. It's going to be angry; cranky someone woke it up, and will want to show us. Some of us will pay the price."

A growl bore its way up through the hard, dry earth. Something struck the fifty-foot high steel gate.

"Showtime," Keekee said.

North Korean mountains are unforgiving: Great upheavals of granitic gneiss, the peaks reaching up toward skies that don't care a wit about political orientation or latitudinal parallels that separate them. The crew stood in the shadow of a sheer cliff face where a titanic opening had been blown out of the rock. But the cavity remained invisible to the humans outside the huge man-made cave because of the towering steel gateway blocking the mouth, keeping all out and something in.

Keekee's crew manned the gigantic retrofitted tractor engines driving the massive spindles gathering up the chains that most likely once clutched anchors from battleships. It was all part of the mechanism that would free the creature for its camera time.

The chains screeched. The huge doors, stubborn in their colossal mass, answered. Something answered from within.

More rumbles, the needles flinching all over the graph on the seismograph.

There were shouts from the stunt coordinator and the second unit director--all the name talent had left weeks ago. The crew left to stand behind the camera were much like those Keekee and Yuz had to work with; a few able-bodied conscripts from below the border or among the academic elite who may know a little about filmmaking but had more smarts and were better fed than the average citizen of the North.

Bang!

They were beyond flight, but even the deepest trauma pool ripples. Yuz's intestines eeled about in response to the assault on the towering steel doors. Bang!

When the first bolt gave way, the second unit director froze in his steps, the aviator glasses he'd likely stolen off a dead pilot reflected the six-inch steel crumpling like aluminum foil; the hopeful reflection of a future in Hollywood failed. He barked at Keekee from where he stood, riveted into the rocky clay.

More monstrous strikes against the huge cage doors. Yuz pulled his hands from his ears to translate for Keekee.

"Yeah, yeah," Keekee said, pulling his own fingers from his ears. "Forget about the door service; hurry, and have its lunch ready, sure, why not? It won't work, but, you know...it could save our lives."

Keekee twirled a finger in the air sharing a glance with his stricken forge master (another ignorant conscript), who stood at the ready with fire-retardant gloves holding the release for the mini forge's pour gate.

Several Shanghai-ed grips cried out and fled. The local Party secretary, who looked on stoically from a lawn chair at the top of a rocky rise, signaled to the phalanx of riflemen that followed him about. They shot in the air. The creature screamed in return. More unconsenting workers fled. The soldiers picked one and shot him dead. The creature stomped inside the cave, nearly shaking the Party secretary from his chair. The soldiers fired again. Another bolt gave way, shooting across the hollow where they had set up production, setting up a plume of dry dirt right in front of the mobile firing squad. A man screamed and hit the ground. The first door gave, thumping to the ground in slow motion. Weak and sickly crewmembers, completely undeterred by the guns, abandoned the shoot. They would be replaced or recaptured, Yuz knew.

If we survive, he thought.

A claw with talons as long as the ribs of an umbrella curled around the remaining door, gripping hard and rattling the barrier. Another rivet popped. Yuz followed it to the rise where the column of soldiers stood with their rifles shouldered. Part of Yuz wanted to call them to shoot at the beast, but he knew it was no use. Safer to shoot at half-starved citizen conscripts.

It was remarkable, Yuz mused, *how unconcerned the soldiers and the local Party secretary took the imminent escape of the mammoth, moody lizard. How much trust they have in our abilities to redirect the monster.* But Yuz thought better; no, sadists do well in a dictatorship and impending carnage was bound to be yummy to their palates.

The molten metal leaked a bit from the large pour cup, making the brimming casting bottle look like an old man at a urinal trying to wait out his prostate. But when the other half of the barrier gave, Keekee belted out the order to pour away.

The second door crumpled, and Yuz commanded himself to stay put, stay strong. He did not care if the film got made, though he prayed himself to sleep every night that the high chancellor's sacred second unit director would proclaim the film done, that they got all the shots of mad monster action as they could use, and released the conscripts.

No, Yuz held his position because to flee would only mean they would all die. He could not let the other innocent slaves to bug cinema perish under the claws of chancellor Il's pet demon.

The cave mouth yawned wide and in its precipice a bipedal serpent flexed its talons, victorious at the defeat of weak vassals daring to keep the committee chair on dino-monster affairs sequestered.

"Let it pour, God-damn-you!"

Yuz abandoned the useless seismograph (they knew where it was alright) and grabbing one of the series of digging tools lying about--a hoe--began cutting pathways in the thin layer of clay barley smoothing over the chunks of granite loosed into the subsoil by Precambrian volcanic ruptures. He made a ductwork of indentations in the ground right through the miniature town the beast was supposed to trample.

The reptilian creature stomped forward, the Jesus lizard of the Agitation Department.

Yuz had all the experience one could want in monitoring and wrangling impossible creatures fresh out of cretaceous purgatory, yet stood transfixed at the sight of the monster. If

three men stood stacked one-a-top of one another, this thing would still have to bend down to pet the top one on the head like a child, stroking him with hideous, unforgiving claws. The thing's tail snaked behind like a bridezilla's veil, except this limb wriggled and reached with its own serpentine intent.

Worst of all, stranger still than eyeballing an image thrown back to a Jurassic Thursday of little note except that every little thing, every creature great and small, were monsters, stranger still was that this animal had a special adaptation that seemed more magic than biology. Rippling along its back and down to the tip of the tail, the scales shimmered so vigorously, with such reflective, molecular synchronicity that it was impossible to tell where the thing's dorsal region ended and the mouth of the cave began. The monster, the Bulgasari, merged, from the observer's perspective, with the surrounding environment.

Yuz shook himself free of the perpetual shock instilled by a Korean Godzilla come to life when he smelled rubber and felt warm soup pouring into his military issue boots. He leapt back away from the stream of molten metal seeping past his left foot.

The burning streams lit the creature's path and blocked it from easy access to wreaking devastation on the little beings that dared to cage it. And it was these red hot streams that were the crew's only defense, not because of the nasty heat of the steel tributaries, but because of all the inexplicable unlikelihoods pasting Yuz in the face, he knew the thing loved to lap at puddles of hot metal.

But I wouldn't bet my life on it behaving today, Yuz thought to himself. *It woke up mad.*

Much of the crew brought over the border with him had perished. Doyoon had been sent back to the parallel and released after getting some mysterious illness that every other person on the crew seemed to come down with in the first weeks of production. Chan Hee had

been so successful, the director took her as part of the first unit to the shore to film romantic, silent 'b' roll of the two leads frolicking along the unforgiving Nampo Islet. Too bad they brought her back.

Yuz had fewer worries now. He had shouldered great guilt in the truly awful beginning of this dark adventure. After all, he was the one who had advised his students not to resist, had assured them they would return. Chan Hee would never return. On this top secret, fantastic mission, her body had been a loose end, a political liability of an organic nature. They burned the leftovers from yesterday's shoot at midnight. Still, Yuz wouldn't mind staying alive.

"What is it about this material, about melted metal?" Yuz mused aloud. "The steel doors do not hold the same sort of attraction, as we can see."

Taking it for a conversation, Keekee smacked his lips and answered, "You ever have a cheese sandwich?"

"Of course," Yuz said. "Split kifi with generous slices of fresh mozzarella. Hmm…I sort of wish I was not thinking of this now, not knowing if I will ever again consume anything other than my allotment of nuts and gruel."

The monster moved. It growled. It was a monster. In a moment, something monstrous would happen, of that there was no doubt.

"Well, I'll tell ya mate," Keekee said, "I'd give five cheese sandwiches and your mother's second virginity for a hack at a plate of cheesy scrolls. Don't know what knowledge comes with all those fancy degrees of yours, mate, but I can assure you, some things are just tastier in a melted form."

Yuz chuckled, but in the numb core of the moment, the moment before action leading to sure catastrophe, an empty moment between he and the Australian opened into a pocket of quiet.

"Metals donate, give off electrons," Yuz continued to muse.

Keekee, knowing he was all important in a most tangential way, piped up, "If I get punched in the jaw when I'm bonkers, I taste copper."

"Yes," Yuz said, allowing his mind, which had gone down too few avenues that involved actual contemplation, floated now. "Metals sometimes, often, are superior to other components of an ionic bond, not often, but it happens."

"What's that got to do with the price of tea in…"

No need to complete that sentiment, any number of reasons might qualify, yet...yet...Yuz could not quite complete the thought, but that was fine for the moment, the pause in the tragedy about to unfold, had concluded.

As weak a hope the metal rivulets (first batch steel, giving way to pig iron) in the dirt had been, the monster lizard that walked like a man eyed the tributaries--like a bird considering its seed options from askance--and then strided with mammoth reach toward the paltry simians that dared to act as jailers.

As vicious as the long claws were, and as threatening as the long-toothed leer appeared out of a mouth as alien as a talking alligator, to Yuz, it was all too predictable.

But he hoped all the same. He hoped.

Yuz and the ragtag group that had come to be known as the Department of Containment backed up, locking eyes on the creature, careful not to slip back into a stream of molten metal.

"Get in there and do your job," the second unit director yelled through the megaphone. He was a uniquely small man who had appropriated the tallest of the canvas deck chairs associated with film directors. No matter how tall the chair, however, the second unit's head appeared diminutive; the only association possible was Dorothy's introduction to the land of Oz. "Control and contain! Control and contain!"

Yuz marveled at the little man's failure at pattern recognition. When the thing craved destruction, there was not much one could do to stop it. Luckily, the thing's enmity for people kept it mostly underground. Yuz had often wondered for some time why it ever came out of its own accord. At some point, he had figured it out. This cave, however nice it seemed--Yuz could not judge--it was not this thing's home. It was merely where the military had stuck it once they had gained some degree of control, albeit brief, over the dragon.

Someone got a hard grip on Yuz's shoulder. "Come on," Keekee said. "Let's beat it. This time, at the first sign of the thing overwhelming the troops, we'll run for it. They purposely set up this shoot near the border to keep a fresh stream of kidnapped conscripts streaming in. They knew this thing was fucked from the beginning."

Yuz had no argument for this, no protest. In a way, the dragon, the Bulgasari, represented decades of Party policy that was as strange in its ambition as it was socially catastrophic in its ignorant brutality.

Many of the crew stuck working the shoot were code 139, North Korean descendants of North Korean parents or grandparents who had been found guilty of minor political crimes. Under the three generation rule, the black mark of 139 hung around the necks of now two generations of North Koreans, creating a kind of permanent, criminal underclass, slaves who would forever be working off the debt hanging around their necks since birth.

Yuz stumbled over a loose chunk of slate, evicting his heart from his chest to reside in his throat. Keekee was there to steady him. "You remember that really little 139 guy, Tei Lung Tao?" the Australian asked. "You know--"

"*Just happy to be here*," Yuz said, walking as only Michael Jackson could dance, backwards on a lunar surface. "Yes, I remember."

"And he was, wasn't he?" Keekee said. "He was a true instruction on how the hinterlands of the country must really suffer."

This was all a dance with its own timing. The banter kept their minds cool for what would come next, the plan and all the things the plan would mutate into when the narrative of the caper went awry.

"The great project does come with its compensations," Yuz said. "Three somewhat nutritious meals in a day is more than the average citizenry sees in a week."

It was getting late. They were losing daylight, putting the film crew on edge. The dusk sky had darkened to an impenetrable slate from which a flash of lightning seemed a harbinger of a preemptive nuclear strike from the West. It was just lightning, but the flash painted the grotesque tableaux with a yellow streak of alarm. The Bulgasari was gone.

Just for a moment, not blending or reflecting its surroundings, but seemingly gone. The hungry mouth of the widened cave, the monster mine, for a moment appeared to have spat out its monster, a mouth without its one tooth.

But as the rumble followed up the flesh, the yawning, rapacious maw of dangling icicle teeth that preceded black, empty eyes along a crocodilian snout emerged out of the harsh, dark rock. Not for the first time, Yuz locked gaze with the beast. He almost wished he could say the gaze he shared with the bipedal serpent transmitted hate or evil intent, but he came to believe what those black marbles had offered was something that shook Yuz far more than ill will. The creature saw him and knew him; the ancient Bulgasari (or the awakened fossil as-yet-unknown to sane paleontologists) saw something small. When he helped give it delicious molten metal, Yuz was doing as he should, serving a superior being. When Yuz, as part of the nameless mass of little animals, poked and prodded and limited such a superior creature, it was an insult of universal proportions. But, whether succeed or fail, live or die, cage the creature or not, the monster was something giant and ancient, and Yuz cowered, looking upon the Bulgasari and hating it for all the havoc it had wreaked. He may as well hate the ocean for tidal waves or the sky for torrential rains. It did not give a wit about you and your small ideas of right or wrong, and, certainly, fairness was something small and laughable.

"Do you remember?" Keekee said, apparently not perturbed by the effect of the lightning to add to the monster's air of near omnipotence. Yuz had to shake himself back into the moment, release himself from the hold of the dark marbles assessing him with antediluvian indifference. "What his strategy was for caging the creature, what he was willing to do? And, mate, what it taught us?"

Yuz grunted assent. "Any plan of worth is like an expensive cake," he said. "Many layers."

"Yes, my over-educated chum," Keekee said, his unedited laugh festering into a joyful rasp, "that he did, but more than that, by crumb, you know what I mean."

Keekee, Yuz remembered, was not a gentle man, nor a smooth man, but he was a man of principal. Keekee knew people. He knew people that, perhaps, could have gotten him out of the great project, the message to the masses of the world. He said he had such contacts, a black market trail that led all the way to the western ports of fellow smugglers.

More than that, Keekee had influence, a byproduct of knowing people. He used that, when he felt like trading on his meager influence, to help other slaves to the great movie--a cult film with an actual monster that would meld into some clear metaphor for the cult of capitalism once they had enough footage to get to the editor's booth. Keekee had helped the diminutive man from the inner provinces, Tei Lung Tao (because a Westerner was involved, a necessary nickname evolved). The tiny man, a good chunk under five-foot but in proportions natural to the region, was given the moniker of Lung Fish, shortened still to Fish.

"Yeah," Keekee said. And they both knew why Fish came to mind lately when they faced the monster, a monster closing on them tentatively, maliciously. "Thinking lately about our friend and pretty sure the old fisher had it right, had the answer, by gum."

The impulse was there, by gum. Like standing at the edge of a precipice, the perverse need to jump, to fall free--a fated sort of flying--called to even the most balanced. And no one in camp dragon would come across as balanced to the outside observer. Fish seemed as right as any of them, right up until the time he ran toward the beast instead of away.

Out of the corner of his eye, Yuz caught Keekee leaning the wrong way and had a terrible feeling. He grabbed his friend. "Don't," he said, "please, my friend, please don't leave me alone here."

"It all has to end some time."

FOUR

"Yeah, this is it. We can't go on like this," Keekee said, but relaxing against the pull of Yuz's grip. "Besides, it's not like Fish didn't have a plan. We never talked about it, but in the ol' fisher's last moments, I saw a glint in his eyes."

"Running past the beast and yelling about a cave which we had no power to create does not operate as a plan," Yuz said. "More than that, the thing did not even pay him much mind."

"Not until he started chucking rocks from inside the cave at the thing's shiny back," Keekee said. "One gutsy son of a wallaby. And, more wiley than I gave him credit for."

"We both know," Yuz started to say, but the next step by the creature was far more determined. They had to walk sideways now, an almost crab walk toward the film crew, who, mercifully, held their place (the small chance of getting usable footage trumped a reasonable sense of fear). "We know that a death wish is common in this nightmare, but giving into the impulse is not a sign of bravery or cunning."

Keekee picked up his pace, glancing down occasionally in order to tap dance over the many rivulets of volcanic drool from the forge. "But that doesn't mean we can't form a plan."

Yuz stopped short, careless about his government issued boots. "What are you talking about?"

"A plan, more than a backup plan." The creature demonstrated qualities consistent with the final stages of attack: shivering of its reflective dorsal that would, eventually, build to such a violent spasm it dazzled onlookers, hypnotizing victims so that they never saw the final strike coming.

And yet, it did not seem to prefer flesh as food.

"And you've been constructing this plan, in our desert of thought and inspiration for how long?" Yuz asked, backing up. "Let's get down to the heart of the matter; when, exactly did this plan you allude to solidify in your mind?"

"It had to be somewhere."

Yuz was not sure what his monster mate meant, and, yet, it made too much sense. Kim Jung Il, for all his mystical perversity, did not invent either the ancient myth of the Bulgasari nor bring into being the monster before them, whatever the relation between the two.

Keekee locked eyes with the reptilian gaze. They looked at each other, Australian and monster, each taking long, even breaths, preparing themselves for what would come next.

"Wherever the thing came from," Keekee said, riding some despairing mania, "whatever strange serendipity caused the great leader to believe he could create a movie so unforgettable, so unique...so...as they say, cult, that his ideals would stream along with every VHS view of this crazy endeavor, viral penetration of not just Marx, Kim Jung Sung, but Il himself. Wherever this creature was from, it wants to return, that much is clear."

Keekee grabbed Yuz's shirt roughly to hold his attention just before they took to their heels. "Does it look happy, mate? I have to believe this thing will end."

Yuz tried to muster something to say. He found it difficult to respond in kind to Keekee's rant. He was an imploder, Yuz, not an exploder.

The thing's back shivered, glimmering wave flowing through the rocky hollow.

Then he remembered the deck charges.

"Yes," Yuz said. "My friend, it will end today."

"What---"

But the thing was moving, all the tentativeness gone. It had started its charge.

"If we hold another second," Keekee said, "they may get an action shot."

"To hell with that," Yuz said. "It is not worthy to murder such as the two of us. Besides, I have a daring plan even Fish would applaud."

"Bait?" Keekee asked as they broke into a sideways trot. "Yes, that was the glint, the light bulb I could almost see above poor old Fish's head."

"Perhaps," Yuz said, "but it must be me that it pursues."

"Yuz!"

"Don't worry, old friend," Yuz said, breaking into a full run as he could feel the thunderous tread of the thing on their heels, "I won't allow it to chase me into its cell, the cavern, but you make a good point. It belongs underground; perhaps, it is a matter of degree."

Keekee was breathing hard, looking at Yuz sideways. "I don't--"

"The charges, Mr. Keekee," Yuz said, "the deck charges the effects crew planted along the ridge like gargantuan squibs."

"A film expert now, huh?"

Keekee cried out with wild glee when the creature just missed them with a broad stride of its taloned legs. Melted metal splashed, molten, glowing pellets kicked up onto the creature and the miniature village. Less drawn to the poor snack, the thing opted instead for revenge on its captors. Its tail swept the miniature municipality aside. It was coming for them.

The preferred course, Yuz thought to himself. *The Bulgasari's favorite option. When was the last time it stopped to lap at the steel melt?*

So there would be a matter of enticement at some point in this action, but that was a future problem. Yuz could see time shrinking before them as it did when the action began, the wild, terror-stricken run for survival until the thing got tired and allowed itself to be beaten back by the soldiers' bullets that never penetrated its hide but poked at it forcibly like biting ants.

"Get your crew and get up on the ridge!" Yuz yelled over the pounding footfalls, wild screams, and his own ragged breath.

Keekee, quickly breathless, nodded and veered off while Yuz took a path that brought him over a crisscrossing creek of molten metal, hoping to distract the creature momentarily.

He knew the soldiers would wait to fire.

It was hot, almost mercifully so because they would soon lose the light and the shoot would be done, whether they survived or not, and the frigid mountain night would begin. Yuz danced as best he could between the smoldering streams, missing them but the monster did not. The thing cried out and stuttered to a stop after stepping into a particularly deep puddle of metal. It licked a burned paw.

Then it tasted the metal and it was like a large dog cleaning ice from between its pads after a long winter romp, forked tongue lapping hungrily.

Yuz looked across the rock and mud hollow and caught Keekee's gaze. They exchanged thumbs up as Yuz yelled across to his friend.

"Can you move the charges?" he yelled. Keekee looked confused at first, then another thumbs up.

That was when the second unit director started up with the bullhorn again.

"Shibal!" Yuz screamed back. "It's right there! Right...there! Shoot!"

"More action!" was the return cry but the bullhorn had already devolved into a sort squeaking bats make when trapped in a sack.

This did not please the Bulgasari.

It took one last probing lick of its claws, sucking up strings of cooling, clumping pig iron like a greedy child clearing a plate of noodles, and glared with almost cross-eyed intensity at the second unit director and his screeching bullhorn.

"Joyonghi!" Yuz yelled as he ran toward the light towers and the camera. "Joyonghi Bae. Be quiet. Shut up!"

Taken aback by an affront from what was a clear underling, the assistant to the second rung Zeffirelli ran angrily from behind the lights to defend his lord, the man with sufficient talent to helm mop-up duty for what was quickly adding up to a failed endeavor whose only ambitious feature was to be an off-brand Godzilla movie (productions rather humble in themselves) that accidently might feature footage of an actual monster.

Yuz ran past him, the Bulgasari quick on his heels. The assistant to the diminutive, hand-me-down director, hardly had time to catch the quick vicious movements of the bipedal dragon as it dipped in and out of the shooting lights that were set up to focus on the mouth of the monster pen. Closer to the bank of gleaming spotlights, blind spots were bands of absolute black.

The assistant was sucked up by the Bulgasari in a flash. His scream was brief. Unconsumed sections of assistant to the second unit director fell about Yuz's feet. The bank of lights was next to go.

It was all preamble to Yuz. Though the electric hum of the wiring threatened electrocution, and though the bulbs shattered in a blaze of white hot sparks that competed with the volcanic brilliance of the cooling tributaries of molten metal, Yuz did not slow, running past the production line, leaving the stunned crew in his wake. They were all as good as dead anyway.

This was a whole new experience in calamity.

Now the screams were loud, though often strangled and brief. Yuz knew his destination, and he did not slow enroute.

Even before he crested the rise, both the unit sergeant and the Party representative were bellowing at Yuz, who, from their perspective, had abandoned his post as monster wrangler and was allowing his charge (as though it were a puppy) to run amuck.

What they didn't know was that the Bulgasari, the dragon out of legend, had a special hatred of its handler, and Yuz, normally able to establish some flimsy sort of authority over the beast--a lion tamer if the lions were the size of a city bus--but today he was running and all the predator buttons in the monster came alive with the chase. Whatever damage happened along the way, the Bulgasari wanted Yuz's head between its bone crushing jaws.

Yuz could never understand why the local Party leader had to be present. Chancellor Il had been present a good share of the time while principal photography was recorded by the state-of-the-art Panasonic 35mm cameras. But now it was all clear; the sturdy looking woman who had likely been rising in the ranks of the Party, was placed here to take the blame for the inevitable catastrophe of combining the delicate industry of cinematography and monsters more ancient than the rocks filling the surrounding mountain peaks.

"Yohan!" the Party representative yelled her favorite name for Yuz at the geologist. "You unwanted thing. Keep to your position."

Yuz ran through the production line, creature of ancient legend in tow.

There was no use, of course, figuring on the creature's origins. The conscripts were brought late into the devilish process and curiosity was severely discouraged. Children of both sides of the parallel knew of the Bulgasari. After all, Godzilla was an invention of a damaged sino consciousness whose only surviving impulse from the glorious pre-war days was toward

industrial appropriation of all things Western. And, something the glorious leader had apparently tumbled on: sometimes there is powerful social undercurrent in those things the Westerners referred to as *cult.*

Bounding through the wall of lights and second unit production assistants, some of these ponderings trickled through Yuz. There was nothing to think of now that the quick plan was set into motion and the only thing to do was to go until exhausted to death. Literally.

And yet, Yuz was a scientist, his was a brain that refused to shut down.

An organic creature, as all life on earth is, cannot subsist on molten metal. And though the Bulgasari surely was as unlikely as a creature arriving from outer space, it seemed, somehow, more fantastic to Yuz that this was the self-same creature walked out of legend. Being who he was, Yuz had to bank on a population of subterranean species that had managed to remain hidden from the world in a place that in itself was separate from the world. The enlightened sector of the Jung Dynasty had so successfully brought the North into the most perverse form of industrialization and profound secrecy that one could believe that fantastic creatures roamed the barren countryside. Yuz, while a guest of the North, would not have been surprised to have been nearly trampled by a herd of unicorns, accompanied by a strict dictum of ignorance with proper codification and enumeration.

Something struck Yuz, sending him to the ground, knocking the wind out of him. The slow motion flight was no longer slow motion.

For those stolen from other regions, it was an easy calculation. A quick bullet to the neck beat being munched on, hearing one's bones crunch between dagger teeth, a chew toy for a dragon. One of the other conscripts, a plain dressed man in dirty sweatshirt and jeans, fled, a stream of terror-filled babble trailing behind. This man knocked Yuz over in his panic.

The racks of lights erupted; sparks rained down in volcanic profusion about the fleeing help.

The production crew held their ground, certain in their core that the propaganda ministry--the North's closest thing to Hollywood--would reward any survivor, particularly if they were found alive with monster footage. National heroes of the great production would be awarded a place among the art elite who sit at the right hand of the glorious leader and had all the luxuries and riches one could hope for. Access to a doctor trained in the West would be nice.

Yuz followed the screams for a moment to catch sight of men cowering below dolly carts and boom cranes. But he did not look long. This was all diversionary maneuvers that had occurred to him only in a plan formed moments ago. Sure, there is not much to do during a film shoot; he had no film making training, so Yuz's tasks were mostly of the menial, and, often, meaningless variety. Only when the occasional Party dignitary visited was Yuz trusted to bus tables and other such servile duties appropriate to celebrate (in the most humble of ways of course) the presence of dignitaries. And, naturally, once he was trained in the futile--and often fatal--art of dragon wrangling, Yuz was kept busy, or, more like, worked to death.

Other times, Yuz stood idly by, trying to look busy enough not to be given true slave labor. During these moments he observed and pondered. He had no real hope of escape: The North was a dairy cow with stingy teats in its best years and a barren old witch now. Without provisions, one would starve in a few days in the rugged mountains. He watched though, because there was little else to do but die, slow or fast, take your pick.

Yuz got himself up out of the mud and ran up the rocky rise above the production yard, the only conscript to do this because it took him on a path toward the soldiers. The men with the rifles became instantly wary at Yuz's approach and hefted their large weapons.

There were shouted warnings to retreat. Though a rather lowly, local administrator, the gender-vague official was a Party representative. When she saw that Yuz was not slowing and that the soldiers--who had naturally been absorbed in the monstrous consuming of the production crew--were caught off guard, the administrator showed ample concern.

The first bullet whizzed by Yuz's ear, but he continued his full tilt scramble. The next shot was really wide, but Yuz had anticipated that; he was not committing suicide by Red Guard. No one had worked with the Bulgasari more than Yuz over the last few weeks. He had counted on that in this wild plan, how to time the monster's anger.

The idea that they would leave a Party official with little more than what added up to an inexperienced firing squad, to Yuz, was purely silly, particularly when one calculated the odds. Yuz had time to think about it, and he was forced to conclude that there must be some sort of failsafe built into the process.

Somewhere behind the sparse firing squad, somewhere, as part of the responsibilities of the otherwise ineffectual Party representative, lay a greater tool of intimidation. Yuz was after that. And, ironically, the Bulgasari was his partner in acquiring the unseen object. Surely, they had accounted for the possibility the monster might escape its inexperienced, and incapable, handlers. What if it wandered into the South?

The North was once beautiful. More than that, just beyond the elliptic rises of the adjacent mountains were many fields still expected to produce much after the great industrialization constricted them to sewage fed landing strips. The land had been green, in patches, but was now withering back to bare rock. The great, steel-eating monster sure did not help.

The area behind the stagnant line of communist riflemen, behind the Party rep now falling from her canvas director's chair, sprouted a squat tent from the few patches of meadow-rue surrounding. It was there, Yuz surmised, hid the heavy ordinance so beloved by any true communist.

Yuz slipped up the clay slope; behind him the creature cried in frustration, followed by the mad crash and slap as the

Bulgasari slipped too, perhaps even falling. Yuz did not waste time turning. He knew the creature's pace. Yuz bent his head in determination and kept scrambling.

Time to go home.

FIVE

One of the soldiers had collapsed into a heap. The Bulgasari had never made it this far into the phalanx of human onlookers. Usually, the monster committee did their job and redirected the creature back toward its rocky lair. The other soldiers gave way against the charge of the dragon with the shiny back, some scrambling to get another load into the rifle chamber, some turning and running to join the flocks of fleeing conscripts. But the fallen soldier was just a heap of drab olive flack. Yuz availed himself of this loose soldier--still alive, physically unharmed--grabbing him by the collar and dragging the young man toward the squat tent behind the Party official's fallen canvas chair.

"You're going to be a hero, my friend," he said, as he dragged the boy, pausing in his blubbering. "You'll be remembered."

He didn't seem to care about his legacy, only crying and struggling against the relentless drag toward the treasure behind the curtains of the short tent. Yuz reached out and swept away the curtain, and he was not disappointed. He had no name for the weapon he unveiled. He could probably name five kinds of rock that lay beneath the clay soil supporting the big gun, but he was not a soldier.

"That's why I need you," he told the crumbled mess that Yuz hoped could remember his soldiering. "Now, at attention young man, and show the world what you know about this!"

It was a weapon so large it had its own seat, like a drummer's stool except welded onto the steel frame of the rapid fire gun, all painted olive drab.

"I can't. I can't," cried the boy soldier.

Yuz grunted as he hoisted the smooth-faced, trained killer onto the firing chair.

"Tell me what I must do to help you," Yuz said.

A few yards away, the Bulgasari had skewered a soldier as young as the quacking mass before the geology professor and was lowering him into the killing jaws like a green khaki shish-ka-bob. There was screaming, then there was none. Unconsumed, bloody chunks of olive drab fell with an unimpressive splat.

"I kill traitors to the party, not dragons. Not dragons!" This went on for a while until Yuz slapped the boy hard against the face several times. "No more dragons." This time plaintive and resigned, Yuz turned the broken soldier by the shoulder and managed to get him to focus.

"Tell me about this weapon," Yuz said. The soldier pivoted sadly on the bench and considered the well-oiled ton of steel. "You've fired it, yes? One of the best moments of your life, no doubt."

Still far away, the stilted gaze shifted closer but not present, likely remembering tearing a distant target to pieces with bullets the size of a man's arm.

"Red Star 61," the soldier said, allowing a smooth hand to linger over the steel flesh of the thing. "It can cut through two American tanks and still travel through the hearts of fifty GI Joes if they stood in a line."

There were many things Yuz did not believe about what the young soldier said, but his mind could not help imagining fifty Americans lining up in a convenient row, all the better to be mowed down by the Red Star 61.

"The Americans have the M-50," the soldier now said with pride as he took the grips like a pro and got ready to relive the moment he was allowed to fire this most powerful weapon. "This is a far superior weapon. It is one of the many reasons they fear us."

Yuz slapped the soldier on the back and smiled with genuine warmth and strength, reflecting the kid's patriotic joy and confidence. This dissipated some when a human head, still stuck inside its soldier helmet, rolled next to Yuz's feet. He kicked it away, hoping this would not give the kid an excuse to implode.

"The Americans sent this monster here to end our great nation, do you believe it?" Yuz said. "The great and glorious leader has sent us to record it so the world will know, but now we have a greater mission. We must not let it out of this little valley to destroy all we have built."

The soldier took the firing controls with greater intent.

"Go over to the box and take out a loop of ordinance," the soldier instructed, turning this switch and that toggle and furiously dialing a rotor that turned the muzzle of the metal beast to face the demon of rock and blood and capitalism that was now chomping down on the thorax of a good comrade. "You'll know it. It will look like a chain of soup cans."

There was a locker. Yuz hesitated when the boy used the generic *sangja* instead of the rather more precise *samulham* (case rather than locker) which both momentarily confused the professor and made Yuz worry about the boy's intelligence. But, when Yuz struck the load home, the boy swiveled himself and the angry muzzle of the Red Star 61 around to face the horrendous enemy, showing only patriotic determination and malignant intent.

No sooner had Yuz stumbled with the first cartridges of the initial load than--apparently satisfied with the sound of the load locking into place--the young soldier began firing.

Stove top heat glazed Yuz's face and he fell away.

The Bulgasari cried out. The distant cliff face beyond the monster paid the heaviest price, sending shards of shale in all directions. A large bullet, streaking through the air with a trail of phosphorescence built into the shell so that the triggerman could follow the path of the many hundreds of super bullets that would follow, struck the Bulgasari. That was all Yuz needed. The monster screeched and stumbled back, its legs giving out from under it. Maybe the young soldier felt a flush of satisfaction as the creature bellowed and pawed for purchase on the slippery clay. Yuz knew better. He made sure the 61 had a clean tray of ammunition to pull from and then wheeled about to head onto the next step of the growing plan.

Now there would be time while the monster weapon fought off the monster movie star.

A rifle had been abandoned by one of the soldiers; a young man destined for guard duty in the coal mines once it was discovered that he abandoned a weapon considered more valuable than a cowardly soldier. Yuz helped himself to the rifle just as he had helped himself to the shocked soldier boy. He skidded down the muddy embankment to the floor of the hollow where he broke into a full sprint across the flow of the few workers left on the production. If they got the Bulgasari corralled, all these comrade filmmakers would be replaced.

But there would be no more corralling.

Both Keekee and Yuz's crews overlapped quite a bit, being conscripts all of certain education level and skills. One or two of them may have been missing, but Yuz did not do a head count.

Keekee intercepted him. "Okay," he began before having to bend at the knees to take some deep breaths. "My guys, like all the conscripts around here, have to pull double duty. I made a special point about a week ago of trying to make them specially available to the stunt crew, more in particular the pyrotechnical work."

"The deck charges have been moved and redoubled?"

Keekee nodded. "Just as we thought we would one day," he said. "Except, we won't be using it against the soldiers."

Yuz pointed up at the ridge above the Bulgasari cave. "This will put an end to it though," he said. He turned, witnessing the monster regaining its legs and closing on the young soldier behind the big gun. "We'll get the thing back home and bring the mountain down on top of it."

They both watched as the reptile on two legs bobbed and weaved, taking a shell or two but not surprised now, keeping on its feet quite well.

"I've wondered if it can die," Keekee said. "I'm more than half-convinced it's the same thing, the same dragon from those ancient tales you told. If we're successful, bury it in there, it will just go back to its real home, become one with the rock, sucking the life out of the Korean soil, and waiting to wreak further vengeance on some future generation."

Yuz slapped a consoling hand onto Keekee's wide shoulder. "There are many species as yet uncatalogued in the world, my friend. I too have given into the mystical more than once during our captivity, but in the end, I am a scientist."

"No science can explain this thing."

The 61 tore the gathering gloom with screaming tracers. The cliff face erupted in shards of shale. The Bulgasari was struck in the shoulder, spinning it around. An Olympic boxer, having missed with a mighty swing, continued its spin, stumbling closer to its adversary rather than away. It was close now.

"One way or another," Yuz said, "as of this evening, we are slaves no longer."

The setting sun had taken its last hook west before departing for the night. As it exited from behind the major peak overshadowing the hollow, on its way to the next, smaller peak to bed down for the night, it threw forked bands of orange light down into the hollow where the monster battled the young soldier manning the big gun.

Just as the Bulgasari angled for the final strike on its enemy's entrenched position, the bands of shiny scales shuddered with the thrill of the kill. As the last streaks of daylight struck these humming bits of mirror shards and dragon dust, the monster glowed brightly for just a moment and then erased itself from observation. It disappeared completely. They all froze, including the young soldier, who, a moment later was screaming, seeming to fly through the air as if tugged from the gunner's seat by an invisible wire. He screamed as blood streamed down over a transparent figure that, as the blood outlined it, tossed the soldier to the ground who tried to crawl away but was held in place by the crimson outline. A moment later the sun had forded the distance between peaks and had settled into its night home. A glow remained as the Bulgasari became visible again, standing over the fallen soldier like Tarzan over a defeated lion. Then the reptile bent and tore the head off the boy.

Keekee's men came up on their right, flashlights lit. They had already poured kerosene into the runnels where the molten metal had previously hardened. They lit these and the gloom retreated.

Echoes of the young soldier's screams died as he did. Blood oozed down the rise into the muddy gulch.

All the soldiers and film crew and conscripts had fled into the foothills. The monster committee was alone with the Bulgasari. The creature lapped absently at its bloody jowls with a long, spiked tongue like a dog cleaning its face. Then it looked across the hollow, right at Yuz, locking eyes with the geologist, and in that moment, they were completely alone. The rock monster's black eyes harnessed to the rock scientist's own Korean gaze.

Yuz nodded. *Yes*, he thought. *I am the only one who can do it. I know what you are.*

"I know what you are," he repeated aloud.

"What is it, Kwon?" Keekee asked.

"Never mind that," Yuz said. It was his plan. He was in charge now. "Get with your men and prepare the detonators."

"What are you going to do, exactly?" Keekee said.

Yuz looked away from the stout Australian and reengaged stares with the monster. *I know what you are.*

"Don't worry," Yuz said, "I'm no Lung Fish. I'm going to be careful."

Keekee understood now; it was clear. "See that you are, mate," he said. "See that you are."

Yuz hefted the rifle. He did not know guns. To him it looked sort of like the weapon used to kill JFK. He imagined that it was an updated version of the same, but where the North was concerned, one could not be sure. After all, hadn't the Russians supplied both Oswalt and the North at certain junctures of 20th century?

When Yuz squinted down the barrel, the creature bobbed in and out of the bracket of the sights. He could not keep the hands he had wrapped around the stock from shaking.

The last of Keekee's crew clambered down from the bare rock ridge. They had done a pretty fair job concealing the charges, but Yuz thought he could pick out the imperfections in the blend of slate and crumbling limestone in contrast to the solid granite under the mud. It seemed the Bulgasari did not have a jewel-maker's eye for attention. It wasn't fleeing for the smell of a smithie's molten caldron. The creature didn't care.

All the same, Yuz eyed the weapon sadly. He never pictured holding a device of death, something only built to kill instead of learning, discovering. But it meant his freedom.

Is there such a place as freedom? How quickly before one lost hope. But...but, tonight the dragon would die, whether that meant the Bulgasari or the artistic whim of tyrants, Yuz had had enough of the film production from Hell.

Yuz eyed the Oswald-esque weapon and tossed it to the mud with disgust as the last of the light from the peek-hopping sun abandoned them. But Keekee was ready.

"The secondary light source, gentlemen!" Keekee barked. "We held 'em aside for a purpose."

The stated purpose was that the creature wranglers only worked when the Bulgasari was in the mood and so the conscripts on that duty could help out with other needs. Really, it was all one need for Yuz and Cannady. They had been preparing, for what, they dare not say aloud, for theirs was a captivity so complete, hope had been constricted out of them like a monkey that ran into a python.

Measures and countermeasures, enticements within enticements, the cherry hiding within the chocolate. The monster committee had layers of plans.

"To hell with the pig iron, gents," Keekee yelled to the dark air, split by sudden intrusion of Klieg lights. "Prepare the good stuff, the reserved stock."

These words gave Yuz a second wind, who felt his spirits rise though his resolve had never faltered, true belief fluttered within Yuz at the resuscitation of Keekee's undeniable confidence.

The Kliegs were an emergency measure, to be targets for air support. They struck the clouds now and rained down a cold, bluish glow.

There is no such thing as 'white' gold. Instead, there is a gold alloy with dribblings of palladium that we call white gold (Yuz lectured me as we floated on the gig). No matter how many shots from the .45 Lung Fish fired at the Bulgasari, it had become Yuz's theory that it had been, in fact, the man's white gold wedding band that had driven the creature wild--dragon catnip--that had caused the Bulgasari to forgo all other distractions and hone in on Fish. Focusing on the theory--desperation making prayers into bridges--Yuz had the monster committee, weeks before, canvas all the conscripts for jewelry they'd be willing to give up. Keekee understood. They were there. It was time for a monster opiate.

The collection of precious metals, when worn separately, did not arouse the avarice of their captors. A glob of gold would be too convenient a take and too much of a temptation. In order to keep it out of sight, Yuz had softened and banged out the rings, and necklaces and dental work into a tube the size and shape of a metal leg of a bunk.

In fact, it was now the short leg of his squeaky-springed bunk near where his left leg dangled nightly. It was removed easily enough, and he swiped it up and rejoined the monster committee with it in hand. He took out the dull, military issue knife he was allowed to use as his only tool—good for hammering and chopping, useless for stabbing. He scraped off a layer of paint he washed over the bright metal to make it look like dull, industrial metal. The reaction was immediate.

The Bulgasari, cooing and slurping over its most satisfactory victory, pulverizing the little creature that had been hurting it with the big weapon, stood still and sniffed the air. Yuz could only make this out because of the reflective glow of the Kliegs off the low, passing clouds.

"That's what I thought," Yuz said. "You are like all dictators of the East, you envy the West. Western dragons hoard gold. You want to hoard gold, too. Not at all surprising."

Scrape went the blunted knife. The monster licked its mouth with a slender, forked tongue.

Scrape. Cheap paint flecked off and a dull sheen picked up the melee of lights, flashlights versus Kliegs.

The Bulgasari took a couple of loping steps toward Yuz and the gold tube. Behind Yuz yawned the cave, the failed monster cage.

"Come on, my ugly friend," Yuz said. "We need to establish a degree of momentum."

The next strike of the bad blade against the precious metal pipe brought a spittle of sparks. Too much to resist, the monster leapt into full stride, a wobbly sort of gallop that reminded Yuz of an ostrich if the ostrich were stripped of all its feathers and swapped its head with that of an adder's. The eyes were slitted orbs as black and dead as Kim Il-Sung, the North's first great leader.

Things would tumble quickly now.

Yuz sprinted toward the cave, giving the tube of gold an occasional tap. "Keekee!" Yuz yelled. "Commence with a countdown."

Yuz was not completely sure of the timing, but when the Australian yelled some numbers at his crew, Yuz thought it just fine. "Five, four…"

It would be tight, but that was fine, too.

Yuz could hear the crash of equipment as the Bulgasari leapt the ruins of the production line, gurgling excitedly.

Just three strides away, Yuz thought. *It should be three of its long-legged strides before it's on me. It should be three.*

One thunderous tread, two…

Yuz smelled the bite before he felt it. The coppery stink of the creature's maw, laying open to the air a gullet of unknown age and undigested blood. The pain in his shoulder drove an icy spike of hate right up into Yuz's brain. His feet left the ground. He dropped the cheap knife. He felt his left shoulder open as the creature pulled him from the ground like a wading bird plucking up a frog. His shoulder tore open, and in that moment Yuz felt certain he might lose the arm entirely. He almost dropped the length of gold, thought it might be an okay wrinkle, that if the gold rolled away a bit, the monster would forget about him and drop him, and he might survive this encounter still. Instead, he held tight to the hunk of metal.

Yuz realized it was no time for maybes or ifs. He clutched the pipe tightly in his right hand, the right side free of the creature's grip. Yuz flipped the length in his hand so the longer end was pointing up from his fist like a giant, attacking thumb. Yuz hit something, some solid bit of resistance, too solid. He jabbed around until something gave. Maybe he got an eye. He was falling.

Yuz hit the ground, too weak to support himself. He crumpled.

The monster screamed.

As Keekee ran over and propped him up, Yuz turned and with a bit of amused satisfaction, watched as the Bulgasari danced about, crying and clawing at its right nostril. The metal pipe protruded, and black monster blood trickled down the adder's face.

"Come on, mate," Keekee said. "Gotta get you out of the way."

Yuz clutched at Keekee with his good hand. "No," he said. "Got to get it into the cave and seal it up, for good. No time for me."

The monster managed to get an elongated claw around the pipe and swipe it away from its snout. Disgusted with the prize that had become a weapon, the creature turned its back on the offending pipe and turned toward the thing that had hurt him, the little man thing. In one stride it would step forward and eat up both men.

One of Keekee's crew had recovered the rifle Yuz had taken from the soldier. He stepped between the monster and the leaders of the monster committee and shot at the monster's head.

The thing's skin was as thick and as tough as Kevlar. Yuz wondered if even an impossibly lucky shot to an eye would do the trick. The monster recoiled a bit at the impact of the bullets, but recovered quickly and was on the go. The man was swept up in the jaws of the Bulgasari, but Keekee, knowing he could not move Yuz in time, picked up on his mate's cue and, lowering Yuz to the clay, leapt up, grabbed the rifle, and fired.

He moved away as he fired. He backed into the cave. Lost in a rage, the Bulgasari dropped the body of the last attacker--an insectile nuisance--and trailed Keekee, lowering its snaking neck and pawing the mud in long-taloned anticipation of final revenge.

Oh yeah, the creature knew the Aussie. The stout nuisance was an alpha among the other gnats that managed to keep the great beast at bay. He and Yuz must be leaders among the rest, for who else could manage to fool and cajole so mighty a creature as the Bulgasari?

The monster jostled its reflective back so that its dorsal area went invisible in the unreliable light. Then Keekee and the other monster wranglers were exposed to the trick, a final treachery of the monster, the star of the movie.

Yuz had been waiting. His crew now blended with Keekee's crew. When the creature shivered its magic spine, Yuz allowed his right arm, the signal limb, to twitch.

The Bulgasari completely disappeared.

Perhaps it would have been better if Yuz froze then. It would have been the same timing as a strategic pause, but, instead, he forgot all about the signal limb and screamed; mindlessly, autonomically. Yuz's shoulder screamed back, resisting his attempt to mentally skip out on the whole nightmare.

There was no way Keekee could hit the thing with a weapon that he hadn't been trained on, his target moving and invisible. He fired anyhow and Yuz said a silent prayer to a God he did not believe in. Something moved in the shadows and Yuz shrunk within himself, certain he was about to lose his head. It could have been a breeze kicking up with the air temp dropping at the loss of the sun. It was almost impossible to feel any movement, ascribe to any sound other than the determined hunting of vicious talons, of spearhead teeth.

Keekee kept shooting and with every round, Yuz felt certain he would run out of ammo. Finally, though, Keekee hit something, for the round zipped and whined as it bounced off something close. Then the beast cried out and the blood stink of its maw threatened to smother Yuz. Its anger flared and it lost track over whatever instinct allowed for the strange trait of light-bending eye-trickery.

With a wide swipe of its hemp-cord tail, the Bulgasari reentered visible space, turning toward Keekee, who had just backed into the cave opening.

Yuz lifted his good arm.

"Keekee!" he yelled, each word reverberating through his wound. "Get out of there!"

"This has to end, Kwon!"

But not like this, no not like this. It was Fish all over again, though Yuz had to admit, they were ready for it this time. Hadn't Yuz seen the possibilities when Keekee had been asked to plant the charges? Yuz had known something was up. More than that, he had known the possibility of it because the filmmakers, whether artistic or political, had planned for this too. Today was going to be the last day of the shoot, one way or another.

"Keekee!"

The Australian kept firing the rifle that seemed to never run out of ammo, though the clip descending from the barrel looked rather finite.

The creature screamed and pursued.

"Kwon," Keekee yelled. "Please, let it end. Please."

Yuz gulped down a red-hot wad of pain-filled phlegm and, lifting the hand on the end of the good arm as far as it would go, gave a swirl and yelled, "Fire! Fire it up."

Nothing. A whole world of nothing. A huge sliver of silence that put to rest any notion of help. Yuz did not even know where the detonator was or who was working it.

Then the air went hot, and Yuz was knocked back to the dark mud. Yuz lay flat, held there by pain and exhaustion more than anything. Whatever occurred around him, it was the end. It was fine if the Bulgasari escaped its final imprisonment and returned to devour him. Who would know? Who would care?

He felt a rumble through the thick clay, and he realized he could not hear. He managed to drag himself to a sitting position, his good arm jammed into a tent pole position. Extreme lethargy gummed his eyes shut. When something whizzed by his head, the last little squeeze of adrenaline popped them wide open.

At first the Bulgasari did not seem to notice the mountain falling on it; the thing, trying to suckle every bit of satisfaction out of the kill, closed in on Keekee--the monster tail slashing in anticipation. The Australian backed up.

The monster got hit by a large boulder. Keekee let him have it with what must have been the last round. The vengeful beast turned its back on the falling rock and the rest of the monster wranglers and leapt at Keekee who was ready and fled deeper into the pitch of the open cave mouth. In a moment, both were outside the weak, rebounding glow of the poorly placed Kliegs. The mountain crumbled. Shale shards shot past Yuz. The cave shut like an old man that lost his dentures and was taking his last breath. Flying detritus struck Yuz. One of the other crew dragged him to his feet.

"No."

Yuz was not sure if he said this aloud or not as twenty-tons of rock tumbled down to seal up the tall cave mouth. Yuz's hearing returned a bit so that he could hear the angry, vengeful cry of the creature through the earth-shattering obliteration of the mountain.

Within minutes, the Bulgasari and Keekee were entombed beneath the good work of the monster committee. The shoot was over. It was a wrap.

Maybe Yuz thought he felt some sort of tremor warp up through the local clay that sluiced down into the hollow by a river now long gone, a river made crisp and clear and cold by the sun-defeating mountains. Maybe Yuz felt the last tyrannical complaint of the rock dragon of the North as it was forced to return to its cavern home to join other mighty lizards of times gone by, to become just a piece of rock itself, to become the ground the North was built on, to be new-found fossil of a mythic past the new red myth thought it had buried.

The waves lapped up against the small launch's fiberglass prow, its rhythm the score to an audiobook I felt like I had fallen asleep on and had dreamed a replacement story, one so incredible it was nonsensical to ponder with a dehydrated brain.

"So…" My head bounced and lolled to the gentle surf of the sea that had turned desert dry as the looming storms turned south/southwest of our position. I had forgotten the Korean's name. "Bub, tell me this...you say this thing, the bulbasaur…"

A crazed inner voice giggled at my ridiculous attempt to think while the gear work of rationality was gummed up with trauma.

"Bulgasari," Yuz said.

"Bulba...bulba…" Out loud? In my head? It was manically silly. The waves bobbed, telling me it was okay to be insane. There was plenty of time to ask my question, maybe even to get an answer before I die.

"What is it you wanted to know?" a quiet voice said. He was a soft spoken guy this Korean motherfucker, the one who blew up my life with his radioactive package, the dino-dirty bomb.

"Didn't you say...didn't you say this thing you were taking care of was…what? As high as a basketball backboard?"

"If Lebron James was standing atop of it, yes."

Could be I chuckled at the image of King James standing precariously on top of the thing he had made a long career of crashing.

"But," I started, and my mind managed to focus enough to complete the thought, "But the thing that attacked the *Merrymount*, that took my mates…scuttled my home…"

"Much larger, eh?"

"Yeah," I said. "Like if Lebron was standing on top of the Hindenburg…" More internal, manic laughter.

"The events of the fatal film shoot were some time ago," Yuz said. He had been talking for a while, a day, maybe. Salt has a way of sapping a guy of his sense of life cycles. Wasn't he a full professor in the story that took place almost three decades ago? How old was this bit of kimchi shaped like a slender, unassuming man?

The air rumbled, telling some part of me that cared that storms were returning, even if the storm rocked with an unlikely cadence, like the purr of an old cat on your lap, not the angry hateful buzz of a squall.

He had asked me a question.

"Huh?"

"I asked you…" His voice was cracked with dehydration. How he finished the story I do not know. Or maybe I dreamed that he did. "Do you know the difference between a dinosaur and a dragon?"

Huh?

Then aloud. "Huh?"

"All the dinosaurs are dead," Yuz said. "Dragons can't die."

HELLO LAUNCH. THIS IS THE *FELICITY*. DO YOU REQUIRE ASSISTANCE?

To the deity scolding us from what looked like a U.S. naval vessel, what can a guy say other than "Duh?"

SIX

They attempted to debrief us aboard the *Felicity*, a special mission, re-serviced Coast Guard cutter painted black with no running lights. It looked sort of like the ill-fated Zumwalt class of stealth ships that got decommissioned shortly after being built. The *Felicity* had a light crew, running around the Pacific Theater on some sort of dark mission. The ship had a captain, but you could tell the information officer from Naval Intelligence was running this tub. When they caught the rads pouring off us, their reaction was surprisingly disinterested.

Normally, unknown, radioactive Koreans amounted to a global alarm. Nobody wanted North Korea playing the nuclear game. You'd figure we were evidence the Koreans had smuggled themselves back into the high stakes, global game.

The intelligence agent was good. She was also remarkable in other ways. She was what my father would have called a WAVE. We called them Freedomettes. Bush Senior's war changed it all where women were concerned. She was taller than me and blond. Underneath the khaki slacks bulged the thigh muscles of a woman who had done more than one basic training, pursuing more than one branch of the service. Yet her eyes were creaseless, shining blue marbles, bright with an intense energy that did not put one at ease. She bore the shoulder flags of Lieutenant Commander, and like Yuz, age was a hard thing to pin on her. She looked like a college freshman. She even had dimples. But she had those cruel thighs too, the ones that could turn her feet into weapons, no doubt.

She looked over the slender, radioactive Korean with a certain hunger.

They had fed us fluids dosed with potassium iodide through an IV for days without any clear intention of heading toward port and in no rush to answer any of my questions. Yuz seemed strangely uncurious. No sooner had I sat up in bed for the first time then they hoisted us out of the infirmary and into a little, windowless room. That's where we met the blond Lt.

Commander. They had wrapped us in metallic thermal blankets laced with heavy metals so as to stockade the free radicals oozing out of the Korean (assumed North, I'm sure) and the ensign from a ship sent to the bottom of a sea linked to America's longest, active dispute.

The information officer dropped a folder on the metal desk before us so that it fell open and a picture of my companion floated loose. "Yoo Se Kwon," she said. "South Korean national who studied primarily in the United States, disappeared during a geological dig along parallel 38."

Military records of the region oriented, naturally, in relation to the historic parallel established after the war.

The Lt. Commander continued, leaning over the file she had clearly memorized and swinging her gaze up to pan over our faces, Yuz's worn to a state of sanguine hopelessness. "That was a generation ago," she continued. "Resurfacing briefly in the South and then in the States where you had expended considerable effort to get someone in the state department to listen to your claims of a threat from the North."

"Where I was ignored, shunted away as a nut case, perhaps even as one of Il's spies," Yuz said.

"I assure you, Mr. Kwon," she said, coming to her full height, just a bit taller than my five-foot-six frame. She crossed her arms (muscles bulging below blue dress shirt), looking down on the regretful Korean catch with something like the bemused dispassion one considers a child in mid-tantrum. Yet Yuz was motionless. "I assure you, we take nothing for granted about a Korean self-administering doses of Prussian Blue."

My dehydrated, sickened apathy cracked a bit at this bit of random spat of hue. "What are you talking about?"

"Mr. Yoo," she said, "your finger?"

Yuz, still in the modus of a dejected child, held up an index finger, turning the hand palm-up. He barely flinched when the WAVE jabbed it with a tiny marlinspike she had been secreting in the folds of her dress cuff.

Slowly, a dome of wet something formed over the fingerprint of Yuz's pointer. Then it ran and dropped to the decking of the small room. The liquid that fell to the floor was blue.

She turned to me then. "My name is Lt. Commander Lyons," she said, "and I'm going to save your life, Ensign Pinto."

***

Prussian Blue, the person in the doctor's whites explained, has a long and strange history.

My first reaction was that they were about to fill me up with something from Bob Ross' pallet. The doctor had rolled over an IV cart with a bag of saline dangling from it. She took my arm, slapped on a rubber tourniquet, and started tapping out a vein so she could stick it with a long needle.

"In fact, you are not wrong," the doctor, a wide-hipped Hispanic woman, explained. "It's an oxidized form of ferrous ferrocyanide which--"

"Is my blood going to turn blue?" I asked, glancing at Yuz who had just returned from his private debriefing with Lt. Commander Lyons. "Kinda strange you being a Korean with blue blood."

"I thought he was South Korean," the doctor said.

Yuz smiled that all-knowing quizzical grin of his. "I've spent much of my time these days in the North."

"It's why Naval intelligence knows so much about you...oww!" The reflexively angry look I gave the doctor caused her to chuckle.

"I heard about Mr. Kwon's blood," the doc said.

I looked away from the firehose they had hooked up to my arm. I'm not queasy about needles, but...geez...this was no ordinary IV sliding into my arm. The curvy doc looked like she was getting ready to syphon some purloined gasoline from a Chevy parked outside a WaWa's.

Yuz glared at his own feet as though snakes were coiled around them. The doctor took out an ampule of very dark fluid and introduced it into the intravenous line connected to my arm.

"The eighth landmark on the road to Heaven calls the pilgrim to respond with wonder and awe," Yuz told the fascinating floor.

I had the overwhelming urge to scratch, no, to yank at the garden hose snaking into my arm. "Koreans got a Heaven?" I asked, hoping the curvy doc might knock me out for this. I said as much as she released the tourniquet.

"Two things about Prussian Blue," she said, as she fumbled with the tape affixing the flow tube to my artery. "One thing is, we really are going to be pumping the essential building blocks of a color, a paint I guess, into you. Ferrous ferrocyanide was one of the earliest compounds used to produce the slice of the rainbow we call Prussian Blue. It's also a binding agent for certain kinds of radiation."

"But enough to turn blood blue?" I asked. A great pressure in my arm crawled through me toward my chest.

"We are all curious about Mr. Kwon," the doctor said. "We've been wondering about him for some time."

Maybe they did give me something, or maybe watching an indigo snake plunder my brachial artery made me half crazy.

"Dragons can't die," I said to the deep blue snake, "but I can. Sure this stuff won't kill me? I mean, how is having paint for blood good for you?"

I caught the doc and Yuz exchanging a glance. That's when the Lt. Commander reentered our lives aboard the *Felicity*.

She stepped into the cramped, utilitarian infirmary, her hair tied high on her head in a tight knot sailors would call a monkey fist.

"Sorry to have kept you gentlemen waiting," she said, again referring to what appeared to be a file folder in her hand which she threw on the desk to great effect only to replace the folder with a tablet. She gave the device a few flicks of a stiff index finger as she spoke. "What you claimed to have happened, must have--"

But I could take no more. The road I was being led down, a disciple of the mad Korean geologist on the pathway to monster Heaven, I had to step off. "I don't claim anything," I interrupted. "I want to recant my account of events. I, Ensign Gary Pinto, single-handedly plotted the destruction of the *Merrymount*."

Lyons did not look amused by this, shoving the tablet into an armpit while she crossed her arms to glare at me. "You? You scuttled the *Merrymount*?" She sighed and scratched her head below the monkey fist knot of her golden hair. "Maybe you could tell me, briefly, how you managed that event?"

"Boiler number three has a slow leak, it--"

She stopped me by bringing an open hand down onto the tabletop just in front of me, silencing me and making me jump. "Stop it!" she bellowed. "Just stop it. How big a coward are you, seaman?"

"Coward?" I protested. "I just confessed to high crimes. It could get me life in Portsmouth."

Yuz's soft voice cut through the tension. "The first tenet of the path to Heaven..." he started.

"Oh, please don't," I said. "No more of this nonsense."

"The first tenet is radical acceptance of mystery," Yuz said. "There are things we cannot understand but must follow because to do otherwise is madness. I tried to tell you. There is no escape from the path that has been selected for you, Ensign Gary."

"Dragons don't die," I said.

Yuz nodded.

"Well, I don't know about that," the Lt. Commander said, looking bemusedly between us. "Neither the dragon part nor the idea that it cannot be destroyed."

"So, you believe us?" I asked.

She nodded in Yuz's direction. "Gary, he told you the story of how he met the thing?"

"He did."

"Well, Yuz may have been the leader of a monster committee, but I'm the head of Bulgasari headquarters. You two fellows now officially work for D-A-N-I-C-O," she said. She spun the tablet around to aim it at me. "Just sign here. You can use your finger."

"I got a finger for you," I grumbled.

She chuckled. "Dangerous Anomalous Nuclear Incident Corps," she said. "Could mean lots of stuff, but these days it means monster patrol."

"Like I said," I continued, "bring on JAG and measure me for a prison cell."

"Ensign--"

"No!" I burst. "No. Really, I mean, what are you saying? What are the choices here? Because I had no choice about the thing destroying my ship, my first meaningful assignment. Once I brought this guy aboard, that's it. I'm stuck chasing monsters in North Korea because of the fate of dragons? At this point I choose to have choice, whatever that means. Count me out."

She thumbed the tablet.

"And what about your family, Ensign?" she asked, flipping it around so I could see the picture of my grandfather she had likely preloaded in prep for this meeting/recruitment session. "No one is talking court martial here but you, Ensign. However, a likely protocol is to ship you home, let you convalescence for a week in Danbury, then ship you back to Cherry Hill where you can look this guy in the eye: Grandpa Morris Hannon Pinto, veteran of Operation Custom Tailor, Haiphon, North Vietnam. You can tell him how you lost your ship."

"I didn't lose the ship," I said, feeling my heart start to throb and my throat clot with emotion. "I was just an ensign."

She leaned into me, my grandfather's image becoming like a second head as she moved his face along hers in obscenely close proximity. "You're the only one alive. You are the only survivor of a ship that went down, sixty-seven souls lost. The Navy has not yet released a cause. *Currently under investigation*. You know what that means?"

I almost jumped when Yuz spoke up. "They wait for you to tell them what happened," he said. "There may be any number of offices attached to the vine that will produce the fruit, but you are the viticulturist who will decide what kind of fruit the vine will bear."

The smile below the blue eyes and lustrous blond hair gathered into the monkey fist was hideous. "Guess when that decision is being made?"

Now.

There was no need to say it. If I had a fate, it was in the hands of this strange, dynamic blond intelligence officer with the hungry, blue eyes.

She had me too. I had been foolish to imagine the worst they could do was to stick me in Portsmouth, and that I robbed them (her) of power by embracing the worst case scenario. But it wasn't the worst, I realized in that moment--and didn't she have my attention, using grandpa's picture to snap me out of my malaise? Being locked away from the world would allow everyone their illusions. I could stew away in a three-by-five cell convinced of my martyrdom and the family would embrace the narrative of poor little door mouse ensign as a patsy for something unknown, some picture drained of color. They could crayon in their own tones. The bigger the attack on smiling Jimmy, the more the monster became the eternally bullying U.S. government.

But how does he sit on grandpa's porch and look him in the eye?

"Boiler you said?" Lyons scoffed, stowing the tablet. "That sounds fine. I'll submit that and have you sitting across from war hero grandpa in two weeks. I bet you swing with those southern Jersey boys who mysteriously drive around with rebel flags in the back of their pick ups, singing along to Luke Bryan. You can get drunk and explain it to them. How long before a secret eats a guy up, huh?"

I sniffed back something. It wasn't a tear. Honest to God. "It's a secret either way."

"Too true," she said, and I could see she was considering her next move when Yuz rolled over on the office chair he had perched on.

"What about its next victims, Iceman?"

Those are Koreans. It was a dark voice, but we all have it, don't we? And it was mine. I eyed Yuz reflexively. Who was he to me, anyway? Suddenly, I felt very far from home. The Pacific Theater was a plum assignment, or so they told me, but there are people like me, somewhere, and I wanted to be with them. They were sane and white and middle class. My grandfather believed in the Red Menace enough to voluntarily join the Navy at the end of an unpopular war.

What do I believe in?

The room waited for me. Not just the people but the very steel of the decking around us. The forced air in the ducts hummed.

"Fuck it," someone said. I think it was me.

The heavy hatch cutting the small room off from the passageway beyond cracked open.

"Commander?" the seaman said to Lyons.

"I'm busy, seaman."

"We got something on SONAR," the seaman with the cap pulled down over his eyes responded. "I think it's your bogey."

Lyons snapped up and followed the junior seaman, tossing back an order our way. "Gentlemen, keep your positions," she said, but then stopped at the hatch. "Second thought; I think you two need to join us on the bridge."

SEVEN

"We got satellite confirmation," a tech blurted at Lyons as she mounted the bridge. One of the men shuffling around the bridge must have been the captain. My continued impression was that the blond Lt. Commander's presence rendered rank meaningless. "A surface mass at least three hundred yards across moving against the wind. Will likely make landfall at Hwanghae Province."

"A populated area?" the intelligence officer asked.

"Hard to tell at this point," the technician said. "No major cities, but cannot confirm the North's relocation plans for villagers in this region."

A tall man with salt-and-pepper, close-cropped hair turned and addressed the shorter woman. "Should we set a course to intercept?"

The 21st century naval bridge is a dim place. In my grandfather's time a man looked out through the glass of the bridge to see the oceans for himself and live by his gut, the beat of the waves as if a lisping cypher, an informant, for what activities land-based organisms experienced as endless waters. Those times are gone.

The scene I walked into was sort of a pantomime of a naval bridge in my father's father's time. There was a man. His hair was grey. He worked on a laptop, several people did. Their uniform shirts were absent of decorations or marks of rank. There were no windows or portals. We could not see the real world directly.

The man with the grey hair stood when Lyons led Yuz and me into the room. My assumption was that he was the captain. He had a gut that spilled over his belt like rising bread dough.

"It crossed the Kuroshio Current like it wasn't there," he reported.

A few of the technicians looked up from their laptops as Lyons glanced over the several monitors mounted into the bulkhead, the only light source in the room. "Our bogey?" she asked.

"No chatter about it," he said, pointing at the center monitor where a scan of the Yellow Sea showed many slow-moving blobs where currents are fed by a series of warming wells of water flowing up from the deep troughs. A slithering trail of yellow snaked through the highway of various blues--the Kuroshio Current.

Cutting through all this was a smaller blob that the computers interpreted for us as clear among all the other hues, moving with grim determination toward the western Korean coast, ignoring the traversing gyrations of the other blobs.

"Can we intercept?" Lyons asked.

The captain tossed his chin in the direction of the monitor. "We're at fifty-three knots now," he said. "We could crank it up to sixty-three, but I don't think we'd fair as well as that thing did across the big current. We may eat up most of our fuel cross-cutting it instead of the standard course requiring us to ride it, tack our way across."

"Just do it."

The old captain with the big gut turned to the only technician looking our way and gave a nod of approval. The *Felicity* was his boat but DANICO was the mission.

I knew what was coming. I turned to Yuz. "It's going to be rough going," I said to him. "How are your sea legs?"

Yuz didn't seem to hear me. "Will we overtake it?"

I shrugged. "Blondie wants to make the sea bend to her will," I said. "Doesn't work like that. So I wouldn't bet my life on it."

Yuz pressed a hand to his forehead. "We can't let it get away," he said. "But I suppose there is little to be done here. I will retire to my bunk. If I can't see the rough patches, I don't have to believe in them."

"Strange philosophy."

"The fourth landmark on the road to Heaven is purging of the soul."

I chuckled a bit. "Oh, you're going to do some purging."

We retired to the shared quarters issued to us as guests of the *Felicity* rather than persons of interest in the destruction of the *Merrymount*. The frame beds mounted to the steel bulkhead were comfortable enough. Yuz, having been issued a Dramamine patch and a bottle of water, curled up with his back to me, his head covered, the occasional burp rolling up out of him. He kept his eyes covered. I read a magazine.

Cherry Hill is a nothing place in the nothing state of New Jersey. For anyone with a certain degree of ability or ambition, a fair amount of restlessness ensues. My father, the real estate agent, was the son of a career Navy man and showed no such restlessness. I remember longing for a life far away, a life that was global in its scope and steeped in the exotic.

Well, I thought, *I got that, didn't I?*

Yuz burped and moaned in response to a series of violent shudders and subtle swayings of the *Felicity* as we cut across a powerful ocean current that didn't like to be thwarted.

Here was an exotic alright. However, it had happened, I got paired with someone who fancied himself a dragon hunter. And, wasn't that exactly what they were doing? After all, I had been there to witness the destruction of the *Merrymount* by something unreal and huge, something with a bit of the reptilian to it. Here they were, cutting through the Yellow Sea after the thing, or they thought they were. It's what little I could glean from the exchange on the bridge.

Damn, it was a hard hitch, riding on a ship without being put to work. Sure, I would bitch as much as the next Popeye about swabbing decks and plunging toilets, greasing the fat bit for the anchor chain and the like. I even did some light mechanical maintenance on some of the commissary appliances, the ice machine being my particular territory. I was the Iceman.

There I was, stuck on my cot while I could hear the rushed tread of seamen on the gangplanks.

Yes, there are long periods at sea where it's just a matter of getting from here to there via a mode of transport that had been replaced, largely, by air travel (at least for your average Joe Landlubber). Somehow, the brass always seemed to keep you busy. Being aboard the tight confines of a ship gave downtime a little extra weight, but you always had your mates.

Aboard the *Felicity*, I had no mates and no duties except to wait until needed. What good I was in a monster chase I did not know.

A seaman of unidentified rank entered.

"We need you up on the deck," he said, then pointed at Yuz's still figure. "Both of you."

I pushed, groaning, to a standing position. Reaching over I touched Yuz's back and said his name. He did not respond. I felt his breathing through my hand.

I turned him toward me. "Yuz."

He was out, his eyes shut tight and covered in a thick crust, glued shut as a fine seepage had leaked from the corner of his eyes while sleeping and solidified to adhere his lids shut. More than tacky, the sticky mass had formed hard, rocky clumps. Crystals protruded from the clumps in irrepressible stalagmites. There was a small spot of vomit on his pillow. Both crystals and sick were an iridescent blue. Yuz moaned.

I shook him, trying to rouse him. "Yuz," I said, then louder, deep concern settling in. "Yuz!"

I wondered briefly before I rushed onto the gangway to look for help if these materials leaking from my Korean bunkmate were radioactive. Or, rather, *how* radioactive. It had occurred to me that where exposure was concerned, it was all a matter of degree now. How much could a guy take and live? Would I still be able to have kids? Even if I walked out of this with a dead monster in tow and was able to have all the radioactive contaminants washed out of my system, what was the risk of cancers down the road?

But that was the key phrase now: *Down the road.*

The hall was empty. The nearest washroom was in the next section. I leapt through the hatchways until I got some water running, trying for a warm flow. Someone had left a towel behind. I grabbed it and soaked it in the water which had just started to grow hot. I soaked it, gave it a quick wringing, and brought it down the hall to our quarters.

Yuz was in a sitting position. He was breathing with some difficulty but did not rub or scratch at the sapphire crust covering his eyes. He seemed to be waiting patiently for assistance.

"Hold on, pal," I said. "Let me see what I can do about this mess."

Wrapping the warm, wet towel around my fingers, I swiped at the crystalline crust.

He said nothing, quietly accepting help. I began to wonder if he could talk, remembering the spot of blue spew on his foam pillow. His ragged breath made me wonder if he would leave these quarters alive. Again, how much radiation did this guy shoot out? I had to trust that the crew of a high tech rig like this one would know, instantly, if there was the free radical version of a Klieg light dousing me in a bath of gamma rays.

And what about this Prussian Blue stuff? How safe was that?

"Yuz," I said.

Nothing.

Though resistant, the tacky, translucent (almost glowing) crust gave way in adhesive strips until his eyes were mostly clear. Exuding his usual patience (or too weak to do otherwise), Yuz kept his eyes shut.

"Yuz."

At last he opened his eyes, blinking where he needed to, but did not speak.

"Hey," I said, placing a hand on his shoulder, ready to shake him sensible if need be, "you okay, my friend?"

He kept blinking and raised a hand, but instead of rubbing at his sticky eyes, he placed a soft, weak hand on mine. "Take all your sins. Take all your sins, write them down. Write your sins on thin parchment. Fold it; neatly fold it using five folds. Take the folded paper and burn it at sundown on a night where the moon rises late and is big at the horizon."

"Hey, I think we need to--"

The hand was not so weak now as it gripped my hand, vice-like. "Your sins will fly. You will watch them float into the starless night and the moon will refuse to rise above the horizon where it is big and hungry."

He turned to me, looking weak and maybe a bit mad.

"They need us on the bridge," I said. It was a fact. It was all I had in response to hungry moons.

Yuz nodded. "We must go on," he said, "lack of hope is no excuse."

His morbid mood--weird crystal goop or not--struck a perverse chord in me. "If I had known," I said, genuinely chuckling, "if I had known what a downer you are, I wouldn't have pulled you out of the drink."

Yuz smiled at this. The grip on my hand eased. He patted my hand. "Jimmy, your wonderful sense of humor will help you; your refusal to believe will likely save you."

"You guys coming or what?" The seaman had poked his head into our quarters without me noticing. "You've met her haven't you, the Lt. Commander? Don't get me in trouble with her, please."

Yuz and I looked at each other. He took a deep breath and stretched some muscles. "Well," he said, "we have a field general. It was a strong and determined general that first battled the Bulgasari."

"How'd that go?" I asked.

Yuz said nothing.

There are women on ships, sure there are. I've worked with a few, but the more of them there are, the more special and conspiratorially intimate talk between males has become.

"Yuz," I said, "I'm going to drag you the heck out of these pitiful quarters to get you up on the bridge, pronto, but it's got nothing to do with historic field generals battling mythical creatures."

Yuz looked at me. "Please," he said, "share with me the wisdom of the Cherry."

It took me a moment to realize what ethnic flavor Yuz was trying to scoop out of a guy named Jimmy Pinto.

"Well," I said, the chuckle lingering, "the urgency here has little to do with Cherry Hill, New Jersey, and more to do with a basic fact of life, my friend."

Yuz signaled he was ready to stand. I lifted him, and he straightened to an upright position of remarkably good posture.

"Go, on my friend," he said and then added, "Iceman."

"Are you kidding?" I asked. "A man of your experience? Surely life teaches us the same lesson. When the woman in charge calls, a man is foolish to hesitate."

***

The *Felicity* was a quiet vessel. She took the waves well. We were through the current, but I could hear the wind whipping up for a blow. Even the many bulkheads cutting us off from the conditions could not silence the quarrel between sea and sky. The *Felicity* was a special ship, and she refused to rock for anything short of full out squall. Even so, Yuz looked like he was going to hurl more blue stuff.

The dim, tech cave that was the bridge was abuzz. The clear spot filled almost all of the main screen, a tech having zoomed into this mark on the satellite image. A flank of black masses lined the northern lip of the amorphous mass of translucent swirls. We approached from the south, our bearing north/northwest.

“What do you think?” Lyons asked the captain. Her eyes were stuck to the screen.

The captain pointed at the dark masses that looked like tumors growing on the amorphous blob that grew in clarity as the ship’s sonar and radar fed more data to the computer projecting the satellite image to the screens on the bridge. I could start to see bits of junk in the greater blastula of flotsam.

“Those are salvage trawlers, junk scavengers,” he said. “But that bugger there? That’s a different animal.”

“One of theirs, a destroyer?” Lyons asked. “Has it spotted us?”

The captain shook his round head, bald down the middle and ringed with closely trimmed grey. “Not likely,” he said. “The *Felicity* has the radar signature of a dinghy. They probably think we’re another junker that caught some radio chatter about the floating garbage pile, hoping for a find.”

“Let’s stay on the outside,” Lyons said. “What can we do from here?”

“What can’t we do? We’re in range to light up anything you see on that screen. We have a complement of Tomahawk missiles that could fry the whole bunch of them.”

A voice spoke up from my side where Yuz had plopped himself down in a swivel chair anchored to the deck. “We must get in closer,” he said. “We must get in closer and see with our own eyes. The Bulgasari is a master of deception.”

The captain wrinkled up his nose at this. “Last thing we want is to get into range of the deck guns of that destroyer.”

"Hold on, Cap," Lyons said. Then she addressed Yuz. "This thing really is a whole other monster than the one from the film shoot, huh?"

"Same creature," Yuz said. "But with new appetites that have changed it."

It was my turn to point at the screen. "Yeah, geez," I said. "Look at that thing. It's gotta be that whole garbage island, and it really is the size of an island."

"More like a tidal kay," one of the techs said. I could not lock on which one.

"Still big enough," I said. I turned to Yuz. "Maybe we should grease it from here. We get too close and it's the *Merrymount* all over again."

The image on the screen, still a satellite's perspective, had cleared up a heap. Bits of debris formed out of the amorphous mass, the telltale car tires, the door of a fridge, a baby carriage. A field of plastic bags.

"None of it is real," Yuz said.

"What?"

Confused, I looked up to see the bridge had gone quiet, all eyes on Yuz.

"Mr. Yoo, go on," the Lt. Commander said. "This is why I had you brought up to the bridge. You're our special consultant after all."

I looked down at Yuz who suddenly looked so frail, as if there wasn't enough blue left in him to keep him alive. And then I'd be stuck being the special monster consultant.

Yuz cleared his throat and then swallowed hard, as though holding down some blue looking to escape. "You are not aware of it," he said, "but all of you are reacting to the charade. Boats, refuse, ocean; these are not different things but all part of a singular."

"A trap?" the captain asked. "But how? For what?"

Yuz nodded at the screen. "Perhaps no one noted," he said, "but it slowed, allowing us to catch up."

"More than that," a technician added. "The whole mess, ships and all, have come to a dead stop."

Some machine made the most annoying of beeping sounds that I had not noticed until that moment. At first, I wanted to scream for someone to make it stop; surely the friggin' thing could work without making that sound. Then I realized the machine had been squawking the whole time I had regained the bridge. It was just that I hadn't noticed until this moment because the crew had become very quiet. Only Yuz seemed to know what was going on, and we were all waiting with some great anchor of expectation, a kind of horrible paralysis brought upon us by the notion that we all believed in something that was absolutely ridiculous to accept as fact. We lived in a different world now, a parallel existence where monsters are real, and the Korean geologist was our guide.

"We have to get closer," Yuz said. "To spring the trap on our terms."

The captain shook his grey trimmed head vigorously. "Uh-uh," he protested. "I am not bringing this ship in range of that destroyer's guns."

"Maybe we should let the destroyer have it," I said. "Maybe it doesn't have to be a trap for us."

Lt. Commander Lyons fell quiet, working her bottom lip with bright, white teeth. Here was a gal so full of natural authority and confidence in her authority that a bridge full of men bowed to her, and the bridge would be full of the best seamen gathered from several posts and on special duty assignment. These men would have demonstrated their worth several times over, hoping to be tapped for this top secret, all important duty. Or, they were all crazy monster chasers. Either way, it was strange to suddenly see the commanding Lt. Commander (without insignia) hesitant.

Then it clicked. I snapped my fingers before I could think it over. "You've never seen it," I said, the glee at that revelation was also automatic. "You've been chasing this thing for how long, and you've never seen it? Look at this tub, all the tech, and this crew...were you hoping it wasn't real? That's the difference between this crew and me. I know how I got here, and it wasn't because I hoped an oddball assignment might open some doors in the intelligence field."

She looked at me with those blue eyes--cerulean, not Prussian--bright daggers they were, held to my throat. The captain had disappeared from our huddle. Lyons' hands were locked into tight fists beside the powerful thighs hiding below the officer khaki. I thought I could see her start to shake.

Yuz broke this by putting a hand on one of the fists. "Put me on a boat," he said. "A lifeboat, a launch, something small. Let me go to it. I have much more chance of doing it harm alone as this whole vessel."

Though ridiculous, some part of me believed Yuz's incredible assertion. Once you see all your mates destroyed by a dragon disguised as garbage, cynicism cannot get a grip.

But for the Lt. Commander, it was the gentle questioning of her power that broke her paralysis.

"Take us in slow," she said. "Ready the deck guns. As we approach, we'll need a moment-to-moment reconfiguration for Tomahawk launch."

"We'll reach a point of proximity where the missiles will be ruled out," the captain reminded. "Those beauts become worthless within a certain degree of operational incompatibility."

"Blow back?" I asked.

He nodded. "Yes, but more than that," he said. "Use of a Tomahawk fits a rather particular combat model. The salvo arc for precisely targeted weapons like the Tommies is discreet. Helmsman, on my command; confirm? On my command."

But the helmsman, whichever one of the geeks at the computers he was, had already hefted his mouse and drawn an 'X' from our position to the 'X' of a position barely south of the glob of garbage and put in an amount of time it should take. Twenty-first century version of 'ahead, slow'—quarter-mastered by Apple.

We were heading in, to what, hard to say. It seemed that the closer we got, the greater the chance that we could not use our most powerful weapon, the missiles.

Lyons pointed at Yuz and me. "It's fifteen-thirty," she said. "Let's grab a glass and head to the deck."

The captain spun on this. "Sir," he said, "there's a whole list of reasons that would not be a good idea. The glare from the glass could reveal us if we have an exchange with that destroyer, the deck will be no place for--"

She cut him off, the confidence back in her blue eyes. "Captain," she said, "I trust you to keep us from starting a war with a nation that is a newly minted nuclear power."

The captain sighed at this, and his shoulders sank. Some of the gusto left the Lt. Commander's eyes when she saw how much Yuz had to lean on me to get to his feet.

EIGHT

Most seamen have three outfits. Dress whites, or blues, for official ceremonies, anything that might be seen by the public, for really uptight kinds. A seaman will also have casual khakis, maybe two of these if you wanted to stretch out the time between laundry days. And, of course, every sailor has his civvies ready for that day he did not have to think about reverie or swabbing things. True to everything else about the *Felicity*, the outfit Lyons sported as we hit the deck in late afternoon might as well have been issued by the Imperial supply depot aboard the Death Star, severe cross sections of black leather over thermal wear fitted sharply to the waist, broad and angular at the shoulders.

If we were aboard a regular Buckley Class destroyer (about the size of this thing), we would have taken up positions right behind a set of 20mm cannons, close enough to smell the barrel oil. Lyons assured us the weaponry was there, but the deck was solidly plated with black, radar refracting panels. We ensconced ourselves between featureless formations in the deck of random geometric figures. We peeked over the rise of one of these metallic features--surprisingly cool for being black metal sitting out in the sun all day-- and Lyons popped a set of futuristic binoculars up to her eyes. With the naked eye it was next to impossible to discern anything but slate grey waves, dappled with cloud shadow. After many moments of cupping my hands over my eyebrows and squinting, I thought I could make out some solid forms bobbing on the gentle seas. Soon, I could discern the flotsam of the garbage island.

"Looks all legit to me," Lyons said, handing the glass over to me.

I brought the eyepieces up to my face. "It did the last time too," I said. "The *Merrymount* is still sitting at the bottom of the Yellow Sea all the same."

I couldn't see at first, and I could not find the mechanism to refocus the lens barrels for my binocular focal length. Not too surprisingly, the binoculars adjusted themselves, and I was zoomed in on some blinding bit of sky. I scanned down and located the objects on the water.

Three smaller trawlers that looked to be more parts rust than steel floated at the edge of the amoeboid plop of junk. The smaller vessels were all in a neat formation, aligned perfectly with the larger destroyer to form a screen along the northern lip of the junk spot.

It all looked relatively serene, but my heart was beating hard. My mind flashed on the image of the towering garbage dinosaur looming over the *Merrymount*.

"What do you think?" Lyons asked Yuz.

"A ruse," he said. "It is waiting for us, luring us in."

My chest suddenly constricted. I had the distant feeling that history was repeating itself. "Why would it do that?" I asked. "My uncle used to hunt bear, and injured or not, he said the safest move for the animal is retreat, to escape. Facing off, fighting, always costs more."

Yuz nodded vaguely in the direction of the waves. "This no bear, Gary," he said, a sickly sheen glistening on his brow. "It...it…"

I turned in time not to see it, but I could hear him hurling all over the sleek, radar resistant deck. But I had to turn sooner or later, and when I faced forward my stomach instantly tightened and swirled. I put a hand over my mouth, unable to look away from the mess before me, some of it moving.

Specifically, there was a four-inch cone of fleshy substance wriggling in the chunky soup of Yuz's stomach acids. It was slate-grey with swirls of green scales. It was small but clearly reptilian.

"How?" I asked through my fingers. "Why?"

Lt. Commander Marney B. Lyons hunched over to give the mess a more thorough examination. "Ensign Pinto," she said.

"We're not on a first name basis yet?" I pressed my other hand to my forehead, feeling some blend of giddy and queasy.

She ignored this, reaching down as if to sift through the pool of sick with her forefinger. She stopped just short of making contact. "You reported that Mr. Kwon was extracted from the water with a section of flesh from the creature, that it reabsorbed this piece after destroying the *Merrymount*?"

"That's the way it appeared to me," I said.

Yuz remained quiet, resting on his haunches, wiping weakly at his mouth.

"Well," Lyons said, pointing at the living length of tissue wriggling on the wet deck, "does that look familiar?"

It did. It was another piece of the monster.

I turned toward Yuz. "What did you do?" I asked him.

Yuz said nothing.

"It's an awfully tricky beast, isn't it Kwon?" Lyons asked. He looked up at her weakly, squinting into the glare of the leaden sky behind her. "With its unique abilities, it must be awfully difficult to track, particularly in its home territory, up in those barren mountains of the North."

Yuz nodded.

Lyons hoisted the binoculars back up to her eyes but addressed my North Korean pal. "You grabbed that bit of Bulgasari, the bigger one you wrapped up and made off with in order to keep it around, to bring it to you," she said. "You took a bite out of it to ensure the same. I'd love to know how you managed to cut a chunk off the monster. Clearly, it does not digest."

"You had that in you the whole time?" I asked, my stomach doing another flop.

Yuz wiped at his mouth and stood on shaky legs. "I thought it would be more vulnerable away from its home territory. I was wrong."

"I don't know about that," Lyons said. "That garbage patch out there, our monster presumably, was making a beeline for the coast at a pretty frantic pace. Everything feels safer at home."

But it had stopped, motivated by something greater than escape.

"It *is* a trap," I said, a cold certainty taking over. "We have to launch the missiles, launch them now."

Lyons snapped back the binoculars. "We've got a more immediate problem," she said. "The destroyer is heading right for us."

"We better clear the deck before they open up on us with those cannons," I said, forgetting the garbage island for a moment. Lyons shook her head.

"No matter what," she said, "they are unlikely to fire upon us. North Korea essentially remains in a state of cold war with America. They are invested in keeping it cold."

"The captain doesn't think so." I crinkled my nose as the smell of vomit mixed with the clean, salt air.

"We're too close to use the Tomahawks," she said. She looked at Yuz. "Would they do any good?"

Yuz shrugged. "It was the underground nuclear tests that restarted all this," he said. "Woke up the Bulgasari and made it what it is now. Underground detonations harmed the creature. We found living pieces of the beast in the underground facility after it fled, free to rampage across the country. We each took a piece of the section I secured. The dragon started its pursuit with me, a whole new sort of creature, courtesy of the radiation."

We? I thought as my gaze drifted off to the activity of the destroyer. There was something odd about that vessel. I had training in identifying various ships belonging to various navies, concentrating on military craft belonging to sovereigns considered hostile to the United States. North Korea made the list.

Still, the approaching hostile craft--though a darker grey etching against the larger grey of sea and sky—closed, the junkers mysteriously trailing close behind as if tethered to the military craft by some unseen umbilicus.

"Can I see them fancy binoculars?" I asked Lyons. She handed them over.

"They've already stored your focal length and eye width," she said. "Just say aloud 'two'."

I said the number and they adjusted, but rather than being wowed by the space-aged spyglass, I focused my mind, as the robo-noculars had done, upon the approaching destroyer knifing its way through the waves toward us. Except, it wasn't cutting the surf to get to us; it was riding above the waves like on some kind of misshapen pontoons.

My heart sunk, much like the *Merrymount,* which, based upon what I was told, was now some seventy-two hours with Davy Jones and his famous storage unit. My soul was down there with my former ship where I had spent the best five months of my life. I watched the destroyer-shaped thing start to lift from the Yellow Sea on some kind of odd flotation device. The junkers followed in tandem.

"Take a look," I said, holding out the binoculars.

Lyons took them but I ripped them from her grasp, ignorant of her rank or muscular thighs. "No," I said. "Yuz, get up here and look at this."

By the time Yuz creakily dragged himself to his feet, the odd convoy was some ten cables off the port bow, its levitation act discernable with the naked eye. A peculiar hissing sound supervened over the regular wash of open ocean waves.

My heart skipped as Yuz lifted Luke Skywalker's peepers up to his eyes. He scanned the waves as though an Annapolis cadet on a field test. "Uhm," he grunted.

We both locked eyes on the monster wrangler, Lyons and I holding our breath. Yuz gulped. "I believe you should fire the missiles."

The hiss gave way to a great tumult of crashing water, the spouting of a tanker full of ocean geysering toward the sky. It's not seemly for a seaman to flinch at the sound of water movement--no matter how loud--but I flinched.

An alligator wearing a party hat, that was my impression when the Bulgasari lifted its great, new, nuclear-enhanced length out of the sea and ambled toward us like a surfer emerging from the waves after a successful ride. Or, better yet, unsuccessful; it looked angry.

Lyons' neck craned as the creature raised itself above us, still hundreds of yards away-- but filling up the horizon all the same--casting a shadow in all directions. "Uhh..." she muttered.

I grabbed her. "The missiles," I shouted above the continued crash of water off the interminable frame of the Bulgasari. I wrangled the binoculars from Yuz. I played the focus region over the monster that I was sick of meeting. However, this time I wanted to see it, really see the thing that had ruined my life.

Both my eyes and the magic spyglass struggled to bring the picture into focus. Not just the unreality of being attacked by some great, mythical serpent, but the visual vaguery the

Bulgasari created in its super camouflage. Moment-by-moment, the shape of the great lizard's head morphed from something trim like a naval destroyer. All the hours of design that went into the vessel's appearance morphed into the bumpy, irregular surface of something living, of something anciently reptilian, like when you see an alligator at a zoo and are certain you are looking at the modern equivalent of a dinosaur.

"Yes," I said. "The missiles."

All the authority suddenly washed from her, Lyons began to stutter. "But, but, but…" She stumbled. Then she pulled herself back to something adjacent to reality. "We're too close. It would be like throwing a softball in the air and then standing still with your eyes closed, hoping it doesn't hit you on the head."

Yuz managed to get her attention with his first moment of vitality, grabbing her, forcibly, by the forearm. "There is not a choice," he said. "If you are the one to give the command then give it. This is not about self-preservation, nor about the survival of everyone on the Korean peninsula, but of the planet. It is a monster, and it is angry. Weapons of global destruction gave it a rebirth, and it is the world it will punish. Launch the missiles!"

I don't know if it was the crazed look of urgency in his eyes or the way the hand grasping her arm shook, but Lyons lifted her walkie.

"Cap," she said, far more calmly than I could, "you seeing this?"

The voice issuing from the walkie was squawky but clear. "Our bogey wasn't quite what we thought," the cap said.

I glanced beyond the growing mountain of reptilian flesh molding itself back into its true form. The island of garbage--mostly loose plastics--bobbed in the wake of the approaching monster. There was an actual island of garbage, a small realization, but it made me wonder if there had been an actual Korean destroyer, actual junkers. Had the monster polished them off before we arrived? Apparently, we had not intercepted the garbage island, it had been the Korean vessels that caused the monster (disguised as part of the garbage) to stop its journey home. Now our presence in the area attracted the beast, Yuz having stowed the little bit of creature in his stomach, his Prussian Blue-drenched metabolism able to carry the surely radioactive chunk that still wriggled on the deck. It looked like the very tip of the Bulgasari's tail.

"Cap," Lyons said, still cool, "we're going to need some cover but quick. No time for niceties."

The box squawked, "Aye."

The solid, black, steel deck started shifting below our feet. "Come on," Lyons said, pulling us back toward the hatch that had let us out on the empty deck. Mounted deck guns the size of Ford Broncos emerged from the black steel, and, turretting toward the fantastic attacker, began firing what must have been 155millimeter shells. The detonation of the rounds split my head. I may have cried out. These monsters made the 50 caliber dummy rounds we used in war game maneuvers sound like cap guns.

There was a somewhat lesser explosion off the port followed by an ear-ripping scream of anger and pain. The monster, now a massive torso stretching toward the clouds, stopped in its path. The shell had turned it around like a hard open-handed slap to the face, but it was undaunted, soon righting itself and continuing its approach. Lyons pulled us inside the hatch as the next round fired. The hatch handle shook visibly with the detonation.

"You must fire the missiles," Yuz said as Lyons ushered us to the bridge. Occasionally, Yuz had to grasp the Lt. Commander's shoulder for support. She didn't seem to mind.

Lyons did not respond to the admonishment about the missiles. "Come on," she said instead, entering the lift to the bridge and then hoisting Yuz into a chair once there.

"The missiles," Yuz said. I felt his urgency. The 155 mils--still firing forward of our position--caused the decking below our feet to quiver. No one seemed to hear the sickly Korean.

"Status?" Lyons asked the captain.

"Holding it off," he said. "But we're only equipped with so many rounds. Each shell costs as much as a modestly priced home in Nebraska. There's just so much appropriation our contacts in Washington can keep dark."

"What about the Tomahawks?" I asked.

I got back raised eyebrows, and I thought I heard someone titter.

Someone took the time to answer my ignorant shrug. “Long range missile, genius.”

“Are they nuclear?” Yuz asked softly.

The cap and Lyons exchanged glances. “Officially?” Lyons asked. “No. That would be against the Amsterdam Global Nuclear Accord of ‘98. But unofficially…”

There was no need to conclude the statement, and she let it hang in the air.

“It could stop it,” Yuz said. “A nuclear weapon would kill it.”

A panicky tech stood up from his laptop. “How do you know?”

The thunder outside continued; guns called and the creature answered.

“The cannons will run out of shells soon,” Yuz said.

“He’s right,” the captain said. “At least these beauties are self-feeding, no one has to be on deck with that thing out there.”

But we all knew that the monster screams would soon win out over the thunder of ordinance.

The captain sighed, exasperated. “Let’s invite the 50s to the party.”

Techs clacked at laptops. A lighter patter joined the boom of the 155. All this to diminishing effect and little hope, and we all knew it; Yuz and I from firsthand knowledge. The others were part of the new monster committee. They were built to be ready for the fantastic, the deadly.

“Maybe if the targeting for the missile was set to maximum arc,” a tech said. “Straight up and down.”

The captain looked at Lyons who, in return, fixed him with her piercing blues.

“We know our mission,” she said. “To track and eliminate the exo-fuana.”

“*Exo*?” I asked. “It’s not an alien.”

“Whatever it is,” Lyons said. “It’s outside our experience and a global threat. All known life is in danger from this thing.”

Then she turned back to Yuz. "How do you know this will work, the nuke?"

But the thunder went quiet as the priceless artillery ran out.

It fell on me to state the obvious. "No more 155s."

The captain looked at his black shoes with the high shine. "We should make preparations," he said.

Lyons nodded. "We can put the whole tub on remote and control the whole deal from the launch."

"It's happening again," I said.

"What?" Lyons paused to ask.

"I'm about to lose another ship."

An alert jerked out of unseen speakers mounted in the bulkhead. Even before the recorded announcement urged crewmembers to head toward the escape launch, the techs had their laptops (heavy duty military models with securable cases) closed and their stations locked down, all heading toward a single hatch I had yet to utilize.

The patter of the smaller gun outside also petered out.

"You guys head out," the captain said. "I should start the countdown for the Tomahawk."

"Is there more than one?" Yuz asked, hobbling his way toward the hatch.

Lyons placed a helping hand into the crook of Yuz's arm. I suddenly had the idea she would do that even if Yuz was feeling fine. "There are only so many nuclear explosions that can be blamed on the North Koreans, and we wouldn't survive the blast of a double hit," she said. "Come on, Cap, we can work it all remotely from the launch."

"We can't lose the time," he said, fumbling with some rushed keystrokes on the terminal before him. "Remember the mission. It doesn't say about how we get it done or what it costs."

Lyons didn't look happy about this but didn't have a clear argument. She gave Yuz a hoist that caused him to wince some, then looked down at her combat boots rather guiltily. She spoke without looking at the captain. "Carl," she said, "I didn't bring any of you on the mission to die. Start the countdown and get to the launch. There are no martyrs in my show. And it is my show. We'll see you in five?"

Cap nodded and we were off, through the hatch and down an access tube on a metal ladder. We had help from both ends to allow Yuz a soft landing at the end of the ladder. We stepped through a dark passage to another hatch and into the very narrow entryway of another, smaller vessel aboard the *Felicity*.

The techs were already plugged in and had the launch fired up. We were all knocked asunder as something collided with the *Felicity*. The Bulgasari screamed in anger and triumph.

"Let's step it up, people," Lyons barked, straightening herself and dragging Yuz over to a deck-mounted swivel chair.

Mass rumblings and clangings threatened tectonic shifts of a mechanical nature. We were getting underway. I felt useless, relegated to the painfully useless dunsail role. "Dunsail," I said in a tone I thought completely inaudible below the seemingly messy functioning of the smaller ship within the *Felicity*, which, itself, was yet another piece of black ops technology that was both mysterious in its power and the answer to the question middle class Americans ask themselves every payday when they look at their checks and wonder where all their tax dollars go.

"What did you say?" Yuz said, or so I thought I heard above the din.

"I feel so useless," I half-yelled. "Being aboard and not given a role is tough, really tough."

"Dunsail, you said."

I nodded. "It's the sail you never use, or hope never to use, only as a last resort," I said. "Generally, it's a thing a sailor keeps tripping over and cursing on the way to doing necessary jobs."

"But it is there for a reason," Yuz said. "It sounds as though it is held in reserve until its time comes. The dunsail must be there to save the day."

"That's not what a seaman means when he uses the term," I said.

"What about the captain?" someone asked. The other techs paused in their preparations and looked at Lyons. They all looked rather uneasy.

I did too, but it wasn't my captain. I did not know the man the way they did. I could see in their tension that many of these men were Navy.

I could empathize with them, but there was nothing for me to do but be terrorized by the colossal monster descending on the ship. I had only my own thoughts to contend with and the propeller rotor spinning in my head kept revolving, spinning on the difference between something completely useless and something held in reserve of extreme unlikelihoods. Was there a difference? Was there life on Mars, and who cares?

Thankfully, my thoughts were interrupted by something almost as valuable as duty, an order.

Lyons pointed a stiff finger at me. "You two need to get secured, pronto!"

Yuz's swivel had a harness, so did the one next to it. I fell immediately into it and locked myself in.

Everyone just sort of held tight as we were thrust violently forward and a blinding light broke through a field of glass I only came to realize was the fore portal of the launch. We broke the gloom of the *Felicity's* guts to spill out onto the sea, only to have our ears assaulted by the loudest racket yet. I reflexively covered my ears.

"Captain!" a tall tech yelled.

Lyons took my hands from the sides of my head and, likely half-deaf herself, yelled into my face. "The cap launched the missile," she said. "Hope he makes it to a raft."

The next sound pierced my temporary deafness. A vicious, wild cry from the depths of some alien maw cut through the hull of the smaller ship, out-doing the launch of the Tomahawk. Then noises that made my initial hearing loss moot ran my blood cold--the rip and bending tear of something large and metal being attacked. This was it for the *Felicity*.

One of the men left his station as though to leave, no doubt desperately thinking of going back for his captain. Another tech stopped him and sadly guided him back to his station.

The screens in the tight bridge of the launch lit up and offered video from all around the smaller ship, including an image of the sun breaking free of the clouds to shine on the glistening dampness of the great lizard's scaly flesh as it reached down with its hideous claws to rip at the high tech, and very expensive, hide of the *Felicity*--the thing that had sought to harm it and held a small portion of the animal it wanted back.

High above, a brilliant spark of fire burned away the remaining clouds. The monster screamed, and I turned away from the screens.

The explosions from the dying *Felicity* crushed the air from me. I buried my head in my hands.

"We have to get out of range in a hurry," Lyons said.

"But…the cap…" The nearest tech looked up at her with tears brimming in his eyes. She was the boss, but it was clear who had been the heart of the *Felicity*, the dad of the ship.

"We'll have to circle back for him, hope he gets clear," Lyons said. "But we can't do any of that unless we get clear of the blast radius."

"Maybe we should disarm the missile," the tech said. "Let's let the thing have the *Felicity* and it will go away. Then we can recover the captain."

"That's not our mission, Lieutenant," Lyons barked. "Now get us out of here!"

I don't know if it was that tech with his laptop or another that caused us to shoot forward, but I was tossed back and to the right, thrust against the very limit of my restraining harness. The launch was a boat equipped with rockets, apparently.

The horrible cries, the more horrible explosions aboard the mothership that gave birth to the launch hosting us, made me cringe and hold my ears closed. They were distant sounds, left in our wake as we shot along, skimming the waves. The display screens kept the sound alive. I would have cried out for someone to shut down the video displays, but, unlike me, the crew of techs had jobs to do, and as useless as I was, I could, at least, not interfere.

The camera is a poor replacement for the eye. I watched screens displaying the severe talons striking down on the *Felicity* with an inward eye, the clarity of vision only first person experience can provide. The Bulgasari's mass swarmed the ship. The deck beneath us pitched.

Then another sound introduced itself.

Among all the horrible metallic crunching and bass rumblings of the *Felicity*'s boilers exploding, a high, whistling whine knifed through the air.

"Here it comes," a tech said.

"The Tomahawk," Lyons agreed. "Are we going to be out of range?"

"It's going to be tight."

My head spun. A rabbit hole had opened up under me. In that moment, I thought about Cherry Hill, about the endless lines of track houses in a maze of neighborhoods of the same design. My mind leapt to New Jersey, a world away from the Yellow Sea where a small band of people battled a giant reptilian monster with a nuclear missile plummeting from the sky, about to land on their heads.

Sometimes, while hitting the rack aboard the *Merrymount* after a long day of the doldrums, of dead water, of nothing but busy work, and very little of that, I'd find myself wishing for action. Even if it were horrible, it would at least offer a compass direction to a guy's life. Whatever struggles that would happen after war could not measure up.

But this was different.

First off, who would believe any of this shit? In war there is comradery, stories. I don't even know any of these people--as fine as they may be. Out of those positioned on the single cabin workspace, Yuz was my longest acquaintance, a relationship of just under a week. But as I looked at him, his hair quivering with the steady tremor of monster-on-ship violence, I felt as though I was linked to this soft-spoken, slender Korean. He looked up at me then as the whistling whine of the missile grew to ear-splitting intensity. We locked eyes. He had light brown eyes like a bottle of molasses or root beer. He looked up at me with gentle concern with something like pity, but I was not sure what he meant by the look; whether his own wounds and many monster adventures had finally worn him out; or was he directing that pity at me as though to say, *And now you must chase the monster too*?

Except, we both knew I wasn't up to the task, would not hold up on the trail of the beast. In that moment, looking in those soft, puppy-with-an-injury eyes, I hated Yoo Se Kwon.

WHIZZZZZ... WOMP....

Then nothing. The yells and screams struck me first, nails on a chalkboard before getting struck over the back of the head with an encyclopedia set.

The relatively flimsy structures defining the enclosed cabin--resting on a mile of bulbous rubber pontoon--buckled. A window imploded, pegging us with beads of some sort of special safety glass. The smaller vessel lurched heavily starboard, and I was glad to be strapped into a deck chair. A sudden weight pressed into my right shoulder where Yuz's head rested. He was out, the sudden lurch whiplashing him into a merciful snooze. Blue drool leaked from the corner of his mouth onto the blinding white undershirt the crew of the Felicity had slapped over my torso. There were bits in the drool.

More monster chunks?

We seemed to drive to the right for quite some time, pontoons bending and squealing like the sea was trying to make a balloon animal out of us. Laptops tumbled to the deck, their owners trying to protect them from the invading spray.

Remarkably, we sunk heavier to the starboard, the angry gusts of concussive air renewing its attack. Being the one furthest to the starboard, untethered techs went horizontal above me, their dress shoes with the high shine dangling precipitously just above my head. One secret seaman--for they all wore identical white shirts and sailor blue slacks but without insignia or commendations--lost his grip and fell, nearly stomping my head flat with his high shines.

The Lt. Commander leaped the intervening space, latched onto the jagged edge of a workstation, quick as a lioness, and grabbed the plummeting tech. She grunted at the sudden addition of his mass but held tight.

Then we righted, Lyons and the loose tech striking the deck flat and loud. The wall of water that bulldozed us receded with a loud hiss like the conclusion to an orca show at SeaWorld.

The cabin was soaked. We were soaked. Yuz did not wake.

Lyons was on her feet, ready for more trouble. "Radar!" she bellowed. "Someone get up on their fucking Florsheims and tell me if that thing is still out there."

We listened intently to the subtle noises of the recovering launch and the calming seas beyond.

The tech Lyons had rescued tabled his laptop and swept away a sheen of moisture. He scrambled around to plug it back into whatever systems were ship-wide, whatever radar antenna sprouted from the shell between fat pontoons.

He grunted, picking up the mobile computer to shake out a thimble full of water from between the keys and from inside the casing. He had to pause to swipe at a similar depth of dew on his thick-framed glasses. Other techs were up and doing the same, but this guy seemed the most recovered. Lyons and my attention were locked on him.

I tried to stir Yuz with a shake of his shoulder. He did not respond. I reached down and gave his face a pat.

"Yuz," I said. "Come on. The worst is over. Come on, pal. You'll want to see the end of your monster. Yuz."

It wasn't his name. It occurred to me that was why he did not respond.

"Commander," the tech said, getting nose-to-nose with his screen. "I got it."

I gave Yuz a more powerful shrug. His head jumped off my shoulder and fell back, his cheek sliding slowly to my chest. A gurgling sound escaped him and a thicker stream of drool sloughed into my lap, the pre-birth to the chunk of blue meat that slid down my chest into the blue puddle gathering at my crotch. Yuz's face fell into the puddle as he went completely limp. I brought two fingers up to his neck to look for a pulse. His neck was as lifeless as the lump of Bulgasari gathering in the lap of the sweats issued me.

"He's dead," I told the room, but everyone was locked onto what the tech with the radar read said next.

Blue ichor and bits of the beast Yuz had swallowed continued to leak out of his mouth. Presumably, he had consumed creature bits to keep it looking for him rather than roaming the countryside killing more Koreans.

I felt my gorge rise. I tried to clamp it with a hand.

The tech stood suddenly straight. "It's uh…"

The beat between this incomplete statement and Lyon's reaction seemed an eternity.

"Yes?" Lyons asked. "It's…?"

The tech straightened his glasses. “It’s right behind us.”

This time the lurch was a massive push from the aft, throwing all the loose techs forward. I saw one of them facialize against the hard edge of a workstation.

I clenched and turned away.

I stayed clenched as I waited for the next blow, the one that would finish this little craft. We all waited, some frozen in place, kneeling or holding their bleeding lips. Lyons bent to attend to the tech with the split lip, removing the black jacket she had worn on deck and using her dress whites (already dotted with blood) to staunch the bloody flow from the man’s face. She left it for him to hold as she scrambled around to check radar screens. When those failed to satisfy her, she bolted out of the cabin and scrambled along the narrow gunwale to the slim dipping platform at the aft.

The eyes of the men followed her. None of them looked grateful for Lyon’s quick, life-saving actions.

I unhooked to follow her, then felt the weight of Yuz’s head in my lap, to remind me I was stuck under a puddle of blue sick and a dead Korean.

“Someone give me a hand?”

NINE

The death blow never came.

An island of refuse followed us, but this floating pile was not a series of discarded plastics. A secondary shockwave (likely the broken mass of the monster striking the water) had propelled us forward and our wake sucked this mess up behind us.

"What are we to do with it?" I said to Lyons as we looked down into the shredded flotsam.

"How many pieces did it break into?" Yuz's hope that drawing the Bulgasari away from land would make it vulnerable had proven true.

We stood at the blown out portal, looking down at it, floating chunks of monster bobbing in the gentle chop. Like so many dismembered grouper, the hunks of various sizes stretched as far as the eye could see, cut short by a growing fog that had crept up on us from the north as the sun was three whistles down and heading to the rack. Gulls had already found the haul of Bulgasari bits, some large enough for them to land on and fruitlessly pick away at the torn edges.

Some bitter members of the crew conjured up memories of their captain. No one mentioned Yuz.

A smiling tech, high on having escaped death, pointed at the blue mess at the crotch of my sweats while giving a head tilt to the floating monster chunks in the water. "We're not going to have to eat those monster fillets, are we?"

He was joking; heck, I laughed a bit at that too. They had been commissioned to chase this thing, the Bulgasari, and I had come across it twice, but none of us had the prolonged exposure as Yuz, the Korean geologist. The whole thing had a dream-like quality for us, particularly for them, these men who had known the Bulgasari as an ugly smudge on their laptop screens, maybe some smuggled video footage in their training. The only one among us to have a prolonged relationship with the creature was wrapped up tight and in a hold below the decking.

Another tech joined in. “Yeah,” he said, chucking the top of the water bottle through the empty window frame at the meaty bits. “I’d have to turn my blood blue so that I could hold monster meat in my gut.”

“Hah, see what it did for the Korean?”

I smiled, but as I looked out over the gentle bulge and swell of the waves, the adrenaline-driven glee fled me. I stared at the ragged chunks of heavily armored serpent meat.

Tastes like chicken, a perverse voice sounded within me.

People moved around me. Lyons wandered by and made some crucial point to me. I only stared at the monster meat as the sun dropped into the western water. Someone thrust a protein bar from a rations kit at me. I still held it as we lost the light.

And, as the sun left for good, wasn’t I sorta sure that the bits were bigger and there were fewer of them? Hadn’t there been some chunks the size of coffee cans and now the smallest was the size of a rottweiler? Then the sun was gone, and I was left with the sound of the slap of the waves against our launch and chunks of monster meat thumping against the hull. The smell told me the chunks were there. It was like being stalked by rotting hamburger.

When Lyons returned, I was more in a disposition to listen.

“It’s okay, you know?” she said. I didn’t know to what she was referring, but an assurance from this impressive, and kinda scary, gal felt like an ironclad guarantee everything would be fine. “You don’t have to watch it. We don’t have any confirmation on the notion that the thing can pull itself together. It was just an animal after all.”

I recalled the destruction of the *Merrymount*. “I saw it,” I said. “It pulled the chunk Yuz carried back into itself, absorbed it like a growing cotton candy ball.”

“Lots of things happened,” she said, a note of consolation in her voice. “Lots of things happened to you.”

“But it happened,” I said, looking out into the black, wondering if I could hear the thing pulling itself back together.

She took me by the shoulder and turned me. I could see her by the emergency lights in the cabin. “Those were your people,” she said. “Those were the trusty shellbacks that took your pollywog ass and slapped a yellow mop brush on your head and called you queen of the sea the moment you crossed the date line."

"You know you're seafaring, huh?" I said. "Wasn't so clear on what branch you affiliate with."

"I affiliate with all of them; got to," she said. "Not you though, you are Navy blue through and through."

"More Prussian Blue now."

We chuckled a bit, not for long. She poked me in my midsection. "Maybe you should go out there and scoop up some monster Scooby Snacks to keep 'em safe in your blue gut."

"Didn't work so well for Yuz."

Lyons said nothing.

A tech from the *Felicity* was at Lyon's port wing. "Uh, Cap...I mean, Commander," he said.

"Yeah?" She turned on him, impatient. "What is it?"

"It's the night watch, ma'am," he said. "Well, you had better come out and see."

My stomach sank, like when I was a kid and I punched my kid sister and had to face my parents. Or, let an easy, soft throw from second sail past me at first, and we lost the game during regionals. I didn't want to move, maybe miss something on the dark waters, as if vigilance could stop bad things from happening. I wanted to believe the monster hunt could end.

But I as I turned away from Lyons, I could see it was far from over; either that or the Martians had landed. A green glow lit the surrounding fog. Either a saucer made a water landing or Korean seas had the oddest dawns after the shortest night or…

I knew. We all did.

I had to hand it to the Lt. Commander. She made me feel safe. Though I didn't want to move, did not want to click away toward the next disaster, I followed her to the aft dipping deck. As I stood alongside her, she stared down into the waves (having grown somewhat in intensity) and surveyed the glowing monster meat as if it weren't the end of the world.

The launch had never been used in action before and Lyons had ordered an inventory of supplies, scrutiny of the four inboard motors, check positions, and reestablish a secure satellite link. Something permanent would have to be done about Yuz, eventually.

I could see as we stood there that the tight monkey fist of a bun had come undone and that a current of regret coursed below her arctic calm.

"Fuck me," she said as she looked down into the glowing blobs.

"Yeah," I said.

"We're all dead," she said.

"Probably."

We both knew the rads coming off of those things would be strong enough to microwave a Hot Pocket.

She didn't move much, just stared. "Should have gotten us as far away from here as possible," she said. "Radiation was a likely danger."

"There were more direct threats to think of."

The launch was afloat, turning slowly on a beam current, casting the monster bits along our starboard-aft.

Were there fewer? Were they larger bits? Was the Bulgasari reconstituting itself?

It didn't have to. Yuz had said nuclear tests had re-awoken the beast, made it the size of a small skyscraper. I had no idea how all that might work, only the fact that a monster got blown to chum and it was glowing as bright as Christmas on Fifth Avenue stuck with me.

"If only we all had Prussian Blue in our systems," Lyons said. Her shoulders slumped, carrying heavily the weight of command.

It slipped out of me before I knew what I meant. "Yuz does."

"Maybe a few well-placed transfusions…"

A seagull called from far away. I guess I was a bit slow. It was only when I locked gaze with those blue eyes that I knew she, in some sense, was serious--at least she thought she was onto something. It was her job to save her men, by whatever means.

"It didn't do Yuz any good," I said.

"We don't know what killed the Korean," she said, a spark returning to her eyes. "I wonder how long it would take to metabolize the Blue."

"What do you…? You mean eat him?"

She shrugged and slapped me on the back. "I don't think the meat will do us much good. But the blood...different story."

"Marney, you can't…"

"Lt. Commander, Ensign," she retorted without much snap. "We've already soaked in a boatload of rads. I gotta do everything I can to stem the tide. Everything."

My right hand looked feeble, reaching out to stop someone who was no longer there. She was gone.

I returned to the monster chunks, looking like waterlogged, washed-out fishmonger rejects, deciding that there were fewer of them, but it was impossible to determine how many had sunk.

Still, I had been pretty sure they had all been, generally speaking, chihuahua-sized. Now, I would measure them up against an equal number of black lab corpses. Details were somewhat apparent in the light of their own gamma ray glow. Some of the smaller features disturbed me. Like, it looked as though one might still have an eye.

I contemplated trying to dig out a heavy duty flashlight to give the meat a closer inspection. A kind of hopeless exhaustion overwhelmed me. Maybe it was better not to know.

They had Yuz draped over a waist-high workstation, his neck bent back and his throat opened. When this position failed to drain all the Blue out of him, they elevated the feet.

We stood around the bucket slowly filling with Prussian Blue blood.

"Will this work?" one tech asked another. The lenses in his thick glasses were cracked. "Does it make any sense? He's dead. What good did it do him?"

Another tech, his dress white shirt ripped to his beltline, snapped his fingers an inch from the other's cracked lenses. "Gotta wake up, mister," he said. "We are way off the rails of sense. I know we signed up for some crazy duty, but it would be okay with me if I lived to see my family."

"Lt. Commander," a tech said, "we're up to a hundred and three rads. We already--"

"Thank you, seaman," Lyons interrupted. "This could do more than just protect us. Once the pigment binds with exposed cells, those cells will be filtered out of our systems. That's what should happen."

Glasses gasped. "Should?"

"Well," Lyons said, "normally, this would be introduced intravenously."

"Introduced?" nervous tech with glasses blurted.

His pal poked him. "No introduction necessary." They exchanged thin, grim smiles.

"Listen," Lyons said, "maybe many of you signed up for this mission without really believing in its target, the shortest path to getting your hands on cutting edge tech, cut your way into decent security clearance for a high paying job in intelligence or the Pentagon. Could be a few of you still don't believe."

A tech with his head wrapped in a large bandage cleared his throat. "Commander," he said, "blue blood and extra chunky, glowing chum does not a monster make."

"For all we know it's just a school of grouper the Tomahawk laid waste."

"Anything radioactive out there is 'cause we made it that way."

"Grouper don't travel in schools," Glasses felt the need to correct.

They were tense and, in many ways, Lyons was not their captain.

She nodded to glasses. "We got a hand counter?"

"Considering our quarry?" he snorted. "Of course."

"Get it."

Glasses set sail for cabinets unknown. The crew stood over the Korean, draining like a spring chicken, the dripping of his blue blood into the pail the only sounds as the men's worn eyes moved from the corpse to the Lt. Commander.

"A captain is his ship," she said.

"Damn straight," a voice said from the mob of bloodied dress shirts.

Then more voices from the knot of seamen.

"Carl Landesteiner would never have ordered the destruction of his ship."

"Did he, Commander?"

Another voice, "Or did you?"

"Lt. Commander," she corrected. "And your captain knew what we were chasing. He knew what was coming. You are all here because of his sacrifice. Much more than his life, he sacrificed his charge, his baby, his partner, the ship."

"Here-here."

Glasses returned with the portable Geiger counter. He turned it on and passed it to the captain. She took it, unhooked the wand and passed it over to Glasses. The ensuing clicking and clacking sounded like Keith Moon on meth. Glasses retracted, scowling. Lyons pushed forward and found another victim, wanding the wounded tech before he could step out of range in the cramped cabin. A grandfather clock with its mainspring sprung, being wound by a child with palsy. She threatened a few more with a wanding, to out them as gamma positive. Instead, she stepped back, and without looking at me, swept the metal wand over my nether regions. The needle jumped a bit, but the noise that resulted sounded like a disheartened cricket trapped in a take-out box, a rather tepid reading. Comparatively, I remained Geiger quiet.

"Gents," she said, straightening away from my relatively radio-inactive crotch and passing her steely blue eyes around the room of men now transfixed by the unswerving will of their commander. "My friends, your only way home is through Prussia."

"Prussia doesn't exist anymore," Glasses said. "The Prussian state was abolished by the Nazis."

There is Prussian Blue, the first artificially created pigment, and there is Lt. Commander Marney Brianne Lyons' eyes. Like the men she stared down now, I'd drink a bucket of the medicinal paint rather than face down the lasers that woman carried above her ruler straight nose.

She locked those eyes on Glasses. "Shut the fuck up and drink if you want to see home again."

TEN

The seas had picked up. A strange front was coming, driven by an inexplicable light at the center of a swirl of clouds gearing up to something just short of a tornado.

And between that light from the sky and the glow of the radioactive beast-a-roni floating by the launch, I could see it happening. I agreed to take night watch, insisted upon it in fact. I could not sleep, not sure if any of our group could. The Bulgasari was reconstituting itself; I was sure of it.

Sometimes you wish you weren't right about some things. There's a great moment of relief when proven a fool. Fools make choices though, and I never had a choice in any of this. Compulsion caused me to watch, playing a flashlight beam over the water to confirm as I saw chunks the size of trashcan lids combine to make sections the size of motorcycles move against the choppy waters to seek each other out.

I went back inside the cabin, what we made into an operations center, to wake Lyons. As soon as I stepped over a prone tech in her direction, she rustled. "Yes?"

"I got bad news."

She sat up, her dress whites dotted with dark drops of normal blood from bloodied noses caused by the missile detonation and ensuing tidal wave. These were overshadowed by the wide streaks of blue where she had drunk deeply of Yuz's blood, hoping-against-hope it would protect her against waves of carcinogenic particles flying off the Bulgasari meat.

I escorted her out to the dipping deck (too small to qualify as a dive deck) and pointed out to the growing waves.

She looked to the sky and the weird, green light first. "Strange skies," she said. "Strange light. Old timers call it eye patch. You know pirates didn't wear eye patches to cover up disfigurement."

I nodded. "They wore them during the day to improve their night vision," I said. "So that patch of light up there. It's the sky looking down on us. Judging us?"

"Or watching out for us."

"You won't think so when you take a good long look out there," I said, indicating the increasing restless seas.

Two or three meaty lengths bobbed up over a wave out of our sight. When returning to our sightline, it was one, much larger section.

"Yuz knew about this," I said. "That's why he ate those bits, and carried that one larger one with him. The Bulgasari can be damaged, and then is driven to reabsorb lost parts."

"It's all lost parts now."

I chewed at the inside of my cheek. "Yeah, but the process is the same," I said. "We should gather some of it up on to the launch and take off."

Lyons was looking at her feet. "Got a problem there," she said. When she saw the troubled look in my eye, she clarified. "Fuel is pretty much gone. We only kept it outfitted for brief shore excursions."

"Seems like this thing was meant for emergencies, like this one," I said. "Seems like you'd want to keep a launch like this one fully outfitted for that reason, eventualities such as our current predicament."

"I had never seen it, you know?" she said. "I saw footage that almost made me laugh except for the look of the five-star general who sat there watching me watch it. I knew that woman, the general, and nothing scared her. It was some kind of footage taken by assets we have in the North who had been smuggling monitoring footage of the new leader's growing nuclear testing facilities. None of their tests are successful. Made sense, you know? Cut off from the world--except China--and impoverished. Hard to build a successful arms program, particularly something as tricky as nukes. I mean half of the Soviet Union's arsenal wasn't operational at the end of the Cold War. But that's not why North Korea's program has been an embarrassing failure--despite what the White House would have us believe."

"It was the Bulgasari," I said.

She nodded. "Nobody knows where it came from, what woke it up," she said. "But it must have been down there in the earth, like Yuz had told you. Underground nuclear detonations are a heck of an alarm clock."

"And its size?" I asked.

She shrugged. “Se Kwon had met with our people,” she said. “Practically harassed us into a meeting. Nobody gets this thing’s metabolism, how it subsists on metal. A lot of science babble was thrown at me, but let’s just say, this thing ain’t built like anything else. It seems to feed on some part of the nuclear device aftermath. And, whatever that is, it’s a heckuva lot more powerful than some pig iron. Something about ions...blah, blah, blah. But the bottom line is, you gotta see it to believe it. I guess if I had seen this thing myself, I would have made sure the launch’s gas tanks were always full.”

“Do the men know that’s why we’re floating out here among all this stuff that’s slowly killing them?”

“They’re not happy with me now,” she said, her face visible in the sickly combined glow of the monster stuff and the eye patch in the sky. “A couple of them got pretty sick on blue blood. I have no clue if it will actually work.”

“Then why do it?”

“Despair is a virus that threatens to infect all of us,” she said. “A strong leader is what keeps it at bay.”

I nodded. “You’ll have to become what they worry about the most. Everywhere you’re asking them to go is the unknown. They, we, must not hesitate.”

She snapped her fingers, grabbed the lengths of her loose blond hair and jammed it back up into a bun, this one considerably more messy than the tight monkey fist she had kept when I first met her.

“Well,” she said, “they had better fear me because I’m not done making demands.”

“You know,” I said, “fear is not the best enticement for everyone.”

Then the most upsetting thing happened. She turned on me in what could easily have been a threatening maneuver--I had seen her in action after all, all those well-trained muscles that rippled beneath her vague naval attire were more than adequate to save techs from plummeting to their death during the nuclear roller coaster ride.

She turned on me and there was a threat that shook me, but not the one I expected.

“And what entices you, Ensign?” she asked. She was an inch taller, but as I locked eyes with her, we were nose-to-nose. As I stared into her piercing blues, the smell of sweat and fear and Prussian vomit might as well have been Chanel. "Would you report me for harassment? I am your superior."

Not sure where I get it from sometimes--I'm not what you would call a clever man--but I do have my moments. "Most women are."

She gave me a questioning look as if I were smart-assing her, and she'd cut me from groin to grin. Instead, she did something that was somehow worse. She dipped down to my level and kissed me. Prussian Blue aftertaste might as well have been sweet wine.

"This is going to be a tough sell," she said. "There are a ship-load of angry, traumatized seamen in there that look at me and see an outsider. All but a few of them are pure Navy, and I'm not their captain. I'd like to know that someone has my back if things break bad."

There was no escaping those eyes. "Sure," I said, hearing the weakness in my response, but Lyons seemed satisfied.

She turned to cross the gunwale and address her men. "Come on," she said. "You gotta help me convince these guys that Yuz's blood was the soup before the meal."

I hadn't seen as much upchucking since my first extended tour on the open seas.

Strange, alright, didn't even taste as bad as I thought it would, but there was a lot of it. A few of us would float out on the life raft that had been secured above this thing's version of an operations room. We'd use short oars to scoop it up into the raft and bring it back in. The bits smelled worse than they tasted. The temperature kept dropping all the while.

The launch rocked as we pulled aboard the hunks we could get loose with the launch's fire axe. From there we went to work with the few pockets knives we had among us. It was slow, painful, gastrointestinal work.

Finally, Mister Chipped Glasses flung his knife aside, nearly knocking his glasses off. "You know what?" he griped. "Fuck this. I mean just…"

He made it out of the operations area to the plastic gunwale and heaved into the Yellow Sea. At least his spew was dotted with much smaller chunks. It would take longer for the monster to pull these pieces together.

Another tech wiped at his mouth. "Haven't recovered from all that blue in me," he said. "There's no way to get all this monster meat in me too."

"Grab your knife, seaman," Lyons said, slurping down a strip of Bulgasari and covering her mouth while it decided which way it wanted to go. "Grab your knife, seaman, and chow down."

"Fuck this," a voice from the door said. It was Sad Glasses. "Done taking orders from this bitch. She don't know what she's doing and she certainly ain't my captain."

Lyons stood straight, drawing a calm hand across her full lips where a bit of monster- riddled drool slathered. "You need to calm down, seaman."

"My name is Rodney Landry," he growled at her. "Lieutenant Commander Landry. Same rank as you so if you--"

FWWPTT!

The launch had a hatchet in its tool chest. Lyons had claimed this when they were fumbling through supplies and parceling them out. It was now lodged between Landry's eyes, the already abused glasses split at the nose bridge, slipping slowly from the lanky man's face. The hatchet blade buried deep in the man's forehead.

The men screamed. They shouted and complained.

"You turned us into fucking vampires, you bitch!" was the only protest I could make out above the din.

Noisy but inarticulate, they were military men driven to primitive rage, cavemen in bloody dress whites.

The nearest salty tech reared up, his knife piercing a vestige of a monster.

Blue ran from Landry's mouth and forehead wound.

Landry's pal reared back as though to strike or complain or vomit more monster bits. Either way, Lyons did not give him the chance to make up his mind. She shot forward, freed him of his pocket knife, and drove it into his neck. Before the other men could react, she cleared the knife--dripping with blue--and cold-cocked the nearest seaman, grabbing him before he could hit the deck and holding the knife to his throat.

The men drove forward. Their eyes were fired with crazed energy, some combination of guilt at having their mutiny uncovered combined with a sick sort of transgressive glee.

"Listen!" Lyons screamed.

Just then a tech who hadn't been in on the festivities climbed up from a utility crawlspace through a section where a floor panel had been removed.

"Hey, good news," he announced, "I think I managed to switch the motor over to pure battery power. Batteries are fully charged. Not enough to get us floating into Osaka, but if we get across the current and into shipping lanes, might flag someone down with a shortwave. If we had remembered the satellite phone...hey, what's going on here?"

Lyons let go of the seamen, lowering the knife. He dropped to the floor in a state of shock.

"Offering a little reminder, a refresher on training, some basics," she said, "some around here need to study up on the chain of command."

There was a retching sound from the back of the group of men. Lyons wiped the blue across her somewhat worn khakis, streaking her leg with a sash of Prussian Blue.

"Maybe," I said. She did not turn. "Maybe we could see how much of the Bulgasari we could stow or tie to the top of the cabin in the raft. Maybe the game now is to see how far we can spread it out. Would likely be beneficial to get some of these pieces back for examination; figure out how to kill this thing for good."

Still at an odd angle to me, she nodded. "Tuck the meat into every corner we got that has a touch of metal. It could slow the rads down a bit."

"The seawater," the guy that just had Lyons' knife at his throat said. "The glowing may indicate that there's more free neutrons emitting from the carcass than gamma. Seawater is an excellent absorber of neutron radiation."

Lyons held out her hand to him. We had emerged from it. Trained to serve not self but country. They knew their role. A gut full of monster can make one forget one's self and one's duty.

"Then we'll sink them," Lyons said. "Tow ropes to drag them underneath the pontoons and lash 'em there."

"Keel haul them," I offered.

Lyons looked at me, smiling, and nodded. She did not look away and that upset me, making the monster bits in my stomach squirm.

Behind Lyons, I could see the men murmuring to each other. A few of them gathered in clumps and eyed the woman commander. They were angry, but they were stuck. The situation required a certain clarity of vision, a plan, and Lyons offered the only plan of action. They may have wanted to split her skull, but that would not fix the threat from the monster bits. I watched the former crew of the *Felicity*, looking for signs of weapons being passed between them.

ELEVEN

Work hard then hit the rack hard. It's a Navy motto, explains a lot of the busy work. Hard days of hauling jammed anchor chain or refurbishing the ship in dry-dock are truly exhausting and lead to heavy, quick sleep in the bunks. That's how it was aboard the pontoon launch that night.

We did it. A plan, a mission, was underway and it was all the bearing we needed to right ourselves. Lassoing monster chunks from both the big launch and the life raft--using the two long pike poles used to assist in mooring--we gaffed the chunks, further gathering them into tighter masses, then securing them by passing the line under the bow and pulling them amidships so they nestled, sunken under that flat, impenetrable rubber of the launch's bottom. The ship's rubbery hull was the reverse pulley we used to leverage the buoyant meat under the vessel. When the pieces appeared to be centered under us like a shattered keel, the job seemed done, and so were we. Lyons perhaps exposed herself as something other than Navy when she dismissed the night watch, but no one complained.

We bunked down among each other, no deck space left without a body covering it. Without long-range radar, Lyons felt better waiting until morning to try the batteries. Plus, the tech who rigged up the motors had also discovered a runner of silicon along the cabin's flight rigging. Having never worked with the launch before, he surmised this to be a solar collector. He too stated he would feel better to get underway in daylight, just in case he was correct about the collectors. Lyons slept right up against me.

Exhaustion combated discomfort as I slipped into a hazy world of half dreams; the Lt. Commander's arm wrapped absentmindedly about my middle, her fingers moving to the gentle bob of the boat on disquiet seas. We lay slightly apart from the others, Lyons having thrown down a pile of tools between us and the rest of the men, a warning system in case they forgot she had saved their lives and wanted to act on simmering resentments.

There could have been a ticking sound from the roof as the dark skies spat down on us. Hard to say what was real. My dreams most certainly wanted Lyon's hand, with her class ring stuck on the ring finger, to touch me with more intent. Maybe she did. My body seemed to react as if she did.

The ticking grew to a steady pattering attack that fell in time with the motions of the vessel. Challenge Grove Park is the smallest park in Cherry Hill, New Jersey. I played there as a kid, as did my older brothers. The seas rocked me there so that I could watch kids clamber among the new, colorful playsets made of composite plastics. Children laughed and slid and jumped, their hair flying in the breeze of their own gleeful momentum. Then I was among them and a small child studied me with a face more akin to an adult masquerading (and not pulling it off) as a child by means of dream magic shrinkage. We played. We laughed. My dream-self thought: it is good not to be a child, but it is fine to visit childhood. Children laugh and children cry and never at their own bidding, under circumstances they cannot envision because they don't understand beyond largely unspoken rules of fun. Then one of them, a girl coming down a red slide, ran into me and bit me, hard, in the thigh. Before I could protest, she did it again, and then someone bit my hand. I fled to a blue, plastic tunnel between amusement stations. The children seemed to have lost me for they were outside, scrambling about, hunting me. It didn't take long for them to find me. I could hear rocks knocking against the outside of the tunnel.

Wack, wack, wack. Louder and louder until I was back on the floor of the pontoon boat, my shoulder sore from the hard deck. Or, did the kids get me with one of the rocks?

The first thing I noticed was that Lyons' hand was gone, but my hard-on was not. I lifted my head. The precipitation striking the roof was louder.

Hail, I figured. *Where was everybody?*

I sat up just in time to see the blond Lt. Commander being dragged out the sliding door to the gunwale. Small, clawed hands held her mouth closed.

Not having eaten and still climbing out of restless sleep, I hesitated, part of me sure this was a dream. But then Lyons shook loose the claw holding her silent and screamed.

"Gary! Help me!"

They did not look very much like the sea-going behemoth that scuttled every ship I had the sorry luck to have sailed upon. Much more like Yuz's account of the beast he faced down and buried at father Il's fateful photoshoot. Three of them, each the size of a large dog, but somewhat anthropoid, like huge monkeys, they had large-jawed lizard heads and scales everywhere.

Lyons struggled against them but this only caused the things' talons to dig deeper, puncturing the khakis, lacerating the dress whites. They shut her up again, roughly. The cabin was empty. These smaller creatures had been working all night. I didn't know what was going on but flung myself forward to stop the beasts from dragging the secretive Lt. Commander out of the sliding bay door to the slippery ledge, and...then?

Where had they come from? There was no time. I wanted to jump and give Lyons a massive bear hug, hold her here, with me. Knock away the mini monsters. But they were fast. I jumped and managed to get hold of one of her boots, no longer brandishing its original, polished luster.

They hissed at me, angry at my intrusion. I didn't slow them much.

"Gary!" She continued to struggle, momentarily freeing her mouth and an arm to strike at the beasts and call to me. I held on, offering some minimal drag.

I climbed up her leg until I gained better purchase, and as we all entered the doorway, I spread out like a spider missing a few limbs, catching my feet on the frame. They dragged at Lyons, tearing at her. She screamed under the claw. They hadn't done any lasting damage yet, but she was a bloody mess. They hissed and used free claws to threaten me. A crash from behind me made me turn.

Another mini Bulgasari had broken through the front glass panel, crashed to the deck, and was now coming toward us. It grabbed for me. I kicked at it, the vessels in my neck throbbing painfully. Fear sent blood through my arteries like water through a firehose.

“Get the fuck off me, you...midget.” I kicked at it. It dug claws into my leg.

I connected and sent the thing reeling. The ones that had Lyons regathered. My intrusion preempting the Shanghai-ing. One of them drove a Ginsu steak knife of a claw in Lyons’ abdomen. The claw at her mouth could not stifle her scream.

The monster opened her like it was slicing a tomato. Guts spiraled out of torn khakis, blue grey coils streaked with red.

“No!” I screamed, but the other one, the new one, had regained itself and was coming for me.

The surgeon among them snipped loose a section of the commander’s freed bowel and pinched out a piece of food that had not wholly digested. Though a red clump, I could see it was a monster bit. This bit fell to the deck and then seemed to, though it’s hard for me now to say for certain, inched toward the monster that freed it and disappeared, the things having reabsorbed the prodigal nugget. The little monster seemed to grow an inch or two.

We had stopped a greater reorganizing of the Bulgasari by tying down the meaty chunks, so instead the dragon went in another direction. Each of these smaller beasts had been a chunk.

Lyons muttered, or her body did. I don’t know; she may have been gone. I lay there, still holding onto the boot. She gurgled out bubbles of frothy blood. Still unsettled by the slugs of Korean dragon working their way through me, my stomach swirled.

There was something once called midget wrestling, and these things looked like wrestlers in miniature with a reptilian team uniform. They had already forgotten about the Lt. Commander and were focused on me. Presumably, they succeeded in dragging the others out into the water, where their sea snake hides gave them the advantage. And no amount of water would stop the dino nuggets from finding their way home to continue to reform, to make themselves whole. To be a giant again.

I managed to get up. The small creatures eyed me, languid hisses leaking out of them as they reset themselves, retargeting. For all I knew, I was the first one they had to face off against that was not asleep, that was upright and ready to rumble.

Ready? Maybe not the right word for how I felt with a gut all full of alien reptile meat wriggling in there like it still lived. But, what else was there to do but to fight, to try and survive?

The hissing grew, but not from inside the cabin. Outside, the rattling of hail falling on the roof lost out to the anxious, hateful lisping complaints of the many mighty miniature Bulgasari mounting the sleek rubber of the sea-wet pontoons. They inched up, eyes locked on me. In the lights from the controls mounted in various parts of the cabin I could see them, and they were in no hurry. Tiny marbles of sky ice pelted them. They did not care. I was the last holdout. All the other humans had been dragged into the sea and freed of their Bulgasari meat. They peered in through the glass panels, their mouths stained blue with flecks of red from men who had not metabolized the Prussian.

Battery power.

There was no way to defeat them except escape them.

More importantly, to prove they exist so that the world powers could dispose of them.

Battery power. They had rigged it for battery power. Who knew for how long, but that was not the effect I was hoping for as I bolted across the room.

These were bad seas. Bad waters, as the old salts would call parts like these. Bad waters I planned on getting free of. It was not a complex operation. It was not a ship. The launch was an emergency contingency that any of the crew could run, even an ensign.

If what the tech said was true, if the engine now ran off battery power (a bank of nickel- plate models primarily used to ignite sparks in the gasoline lines for the big inboard motors) then they shouldn't require any priming or warming up, I figured.

They were scratching at the panels of glass, the little Bulgasari claws, teasing me, toying with me. They had me cornered.

On the long control panel facing the wide, forward portal, I hit the big red button that started up the motors and gunned the ignition. My action had the desired effect.

The launch leapt forward, tossing the Bulgasari off balance, many of them tumbling to the sea and left behind.

The four that had tangled with me remained, three of them the ones that had eviscerated the riveting Marney Lyons. They noted the loss of their companions, now being left in our wake as I steered the launch on generally easterly course. Each minute took us farther from their companions, from the larger bits of itself. If they wanted to gather back into a whole, they'd have a pretty powerful swim ahead of them.

"You wait any longer," I told them hopelessly, "and you're not going to be anything but a bunch of drowning iguanas in a salty soup. You'll be about as far from home as an astronaut in orbit."

They glared at me; tiny, black marble eyes set deep in anaconda faces. They didn't attack, but they didn't flee to try and rejoin with their brethren who were fading back into the salty waves of the Yellow Sea. They didn't communicate with each other, debate the issue. I knew they were of one mind, all small parts of a greater being trying to make itself whole.

Then, as a unit, as the launch bounced over the waves--jostling them but failing to move them--they took a singular, long claw (the Bulgasari equivalent of an index finger), pointed at their own bellies and then pointed at me. They did this in an even cadence, at once, three times.

I nodded and offered my own finger signal. "Fuck you."

They scrambled for the door, their long back claws clacking on the metal decking like a puppy slipping on a linoleum floor except they did not slow. They banged through the sliding door, ignored the gunwale beam and leapt over the side. I could hear the lightest splash over the roar of the motors, eating up whatever juice was in the batteries.

The little monsters were gone, but I got the message. Just as long as I had a chunk of Bulgasari in my guts, this thing between them and me was not done.

***

Trying to tear through the Kuroshio Current is what killed the batteries. They bled out and the sun was up. A lazy mist drifted up from the mounds of pea-sized hail that had piled in the nooks and crannies of the launch's exterior apparatus.

The day was unusually hot, and I quickly looked through the paltry tool locker to see what could help me gather up some of the melting sky ice.

I was not completely alone, after all. There was Yuz and Lyons--what was left of them. It was getting hot in the cabin and my two companions smelled. That meant they would rot as we sat around the now dead vessel waiting to be found. I needed them whole. Not because the smell offended me--there were more disgusting things scattered about that launch than in a hospital laundry room.

The bodies of the remaining members of our monster committee counted as the only proof that any of this happened. I was afraid that Yuz and Lyons would rot faster because of all the Blue in their systems. I needed them to be found with Blue in their systems. Blue blood seemed the best proof of the strange-yet-true.

I took up the deck plating, looking for a section I could completely compartmentalize. The zone that worked the best was a tight series of pipes with conduit breakers on both ends. I stripped both my pals--nearly losing my Bulgasari bits at the smell coming off Yuz.

I stuffed the caked lengths of garment into the breaks in the compartment then dragged the bodies across the short stretch of deck and lay them as gently as I could. They were just bodies; I believed this was true. Yet…

An unusually warm day intruded the cabin. It was autumn and I doubted there would be too many more hot days. Nor did I believe it would take that long to be found. But I needed the bodies to be whole, for them to be checked, looked over, tested. In the aftermath, in the days to come, it would be tough enough to keep sane without having everyone doubt what they really should doubt.

Lowering them, wrapping their arms around each other in a friendly embrace, I poured bits of hail over them. I had to keep them whole, couldn't let the weird Blue advance the rot. I lay down a layer of hail over them as though I was covering them with a comforter on a cold winter's night. It didn't take too long. After all, I am the Iceman.

TWELVE

What can I tell you about Challenge Grove Park? While not large, the green space surrounding the playground and athletic fields offered a nice view of the ponds. The poplar trees lining the nearest pond blossomed with green buds. Can't say I was not glad to be home, and it wasn't like the seas off the Korean peninsula (except for that last day on the pontoon launch) were particularly warm, but I had to hug my coat around me at the tickle of the lightest breeze. Cherry Hill springs took a while to get going.

Six months medical leave went by quickly. I had only two weeks left, and I was considering my options as the sun started to set behind the park. Could not say I knew what was going to happen, but for sure, I was not going to serve again. They were waiting for me out there. I was half a world away and about as safe as I was going to get.

But I knew they were coming for me. Not the Korean monster, no, those who wanted to drag me back into the monster hunt.

The sun dropped as it did every day behind the shivering poplars, the last of the sunlight shimmering across the big pond. As was my routine, I got up from the bench to head up the hill on foot toward the older section of the Haddonfield district. There was a VFW hall up on Kitty Carriage Road. My father had been picking me up from the hall, but it made him sad to see me in the VFW drunk to near collapse pretty much every night. He would bring me home so I could pass out in my childhood bed.

I cleared the dark access road without a sidewalk and was traipsing through the recently gentrified brownstones and old warehouses. There had been something of a tech boom across town when a Chinese firm moved its micro battery design and manufacture shop just outside Philly.

The hall was part of Old Town, not something that could be sectioned off, but rather poked up through the cracks of the new Cherry Hill like weeds.

Flimsy is a word, and the one that best summed up the totality of the VFW's construction. The plastic composite door always felt like it would come off in my hand. It scraped along the concrete, a rasp like the wheeze of a two-pack-a-day smoker. Once through the free-swinging, rusty-hinged door, a warm welcome greeted me. I was like clockwork.

"Iceman!"

"Gary…"

It was a sort of love.

January (Jan) was the bartender. She offered me the perfunctory courtesy. "What'll it be, Gary?" She was already pouring a Bud Light.

Behind the bar was a big mirror. It was one of the few luxuries the manager, Vince Torrington, had been authorized by the local VFW board to install. Etched in one corner was a saying, one of those heartfelt numbers meant to bolster one's resolve. "Calm Seas Don't Make Good Sailors." It sort of went with the familiar Hopper print of the lone oarsman battling rough seas in a rowboat that hung on the opposite wall, a lone nail driven into the Armstrong paneling holding it aloft.

"Watcha up to, Iceman?" Danny Jones asked from my right. "Isn't your time about up? Got the next move figured out?"

I groaned and reached for my drink, tossing a fiver on the bar and thanking Jan. "Don't remind me," I said. "I know I don't want to go back in, but I don't got a leg to stand on."

"Gary," one of the oldsters barely holding onto his stool said, "what's the scuttlebutt?"

They all laughed. "Hey, scuttle that talk."

More laughter. But they all knew. I was aboard not one, but two ships that went to the bottom, that were scuttled. Not a pretty record for a peacetime commission.

"Hey!" a rough voice, a voice half-drowned in beer and bitterness, called across the crook of the bar. "You know you don't belong here."

Harry the Drunk. It was a powerful nickname considering the number of regulars at the hall who occupied the place from sun-up to closing time.

Out of the heavy bodies clad in fatigue jackets and woolen hunting coats, voices came to my support. “Leave him be, Harry.”

“That’s The Torpedo’s grandkid.”

“He just came out of theater.”

“Parked right outside Rocketman, Kim Jung Un’s bunghole.”

Harry rolled off his stool. “Well, you can hang around with a peacetime, wacko of a plebe if you want to,” he said, coming up close to give me the stink eye over his week’s worth of stubble. “Fucking monster hunting. What shit.”

“Hit the road, Harry. You’ve had enough,” Jan said.

The old drunk--a round-shouldered Vietnam Vet--spat on the floor next to my stool.

“You’re a disgrace to The Torpedo,” he said and sidled out the creaky door.

“Well,” Danny said, “Hooah, to you too.”

“Fucking Marines,” someone added.

“Hey,” came the objection.

We laughed. My first was already gone and Jan was pouring another. It was going to be a good night. I felt sure of it.

It wasn’t that anyone else in the bar swallowed my story of the Korean Godzilla--a story I thought I would never tell but the drinking loosened my lips and sunk that ship. But I served and I was a legacy.

Bullshit and beer will set any man straight, as my grandfather (The Torpedo around these parts) was fond of saying.

Then there were shots. Jan joined in, so they became free at some point. Probably explains why we didn’t notice the figures standing at the end of the bar by the door for some time. Danny recoiled as though they were members of the Iraqi Guard. Dan had returned from Desert Storm.

But I get it mixed up. They were there alright, and they might as well have been wearing all the fruit salad of dress ribbons and sashes they’d likely wear for the funeral of a fallen comrade. They reeked of brass. The long, camel-hair coats fell to their knees but did little to hide their importance.

Before the two scowling figures appeared, Danny and I had been in the bathroom. This is when the shots really started piling up. Right on time, as a matter of given course, I lost the contents of my stomach. Danny was next door in a booth in much the same condition except I made sure that I let loose directly into my hands, lacing my fingers together like a catch screen attached to a bailing pump release hose, to make sure nothing of value was lost at sea, or toilet bowl.

One stomach convulsion and a jet of warm amber with chunks of unknown foods streamed through my fingers. The second lurch released the thing from my innards that I refused to lose. I held onto one last part of the Bulgasari.

Danny opened the door to my stall. None of them had locks.

"What a pussy," he said. "Can't hold your...what the hell is that?"

I grinned up at him, wiping at the corner of my vomit-slathered lips with my free hand. It did nothing to help the mess. "What?" I asked, maybe even forgetting about the thing in my hand I held inches above the bilious mess in the bowl. "Oh, you mean my friend here." I stood and left the booth. In the sink, I rinsed off the section of monster the size of a candy bar and proceeded to try and swallow it.

"Whoa," Danny gasped. "Hey, don't do that. What even is that? Looks like a gorilla's toe."

I gagged and hacked up the chunk of Korean monster into my hand, a thin line of yellow drool tethering the chunk to my lips. The bathroom smelled like the diaper of a chimp recently stolen from the wild only to come to live in a lonely old lady's home. The old lady doesn't know the chimp will one day eat her face and shit the remains into the diaper.

I looked at the Bulgasari bit. Danny nailed it. In fact, the gorilla toe appeared to have a nail growing out of it, but I knew differently. This hardened chunk was something special, something cartilaginous like a nail, but essential, maybe even to the creature as a whole--perhaps a piece of the thing's spine. I was sure this piece was important. A certainty lodged in me; the thing would be coming for me, for this last piece. Without it, the Bulgasari could not be whole.

A soprano will lift her head to clear the throat, just as a baby chick will do to accept an over-sized herring from its parent. That's what I did. I looked up at the lowered fluorescent light as I opened my throat and lowered the Bulgasari, meat and bone, deep enough into my throat that I bypassed the gagging response and choked it down.

Danny looked like his nuts were drawing up into his gut. "Why the hell did you do that?"

"Only safe place," I slurred.

"Huh? Safe?"

I held up a finger to stay his objections. "Watch."

I went over to the floor-to-nipple urinal and let loose a stream. It still held a pale blue tint.

"I'm the only safe place for that thing, the gorilla toe. A good name for it," I said, having to hold onto the sink to keep my weaving to a minimum.

"Are you telling me that whole story was true?" Danny asked, a bit more sober. "Geez, it can't be true, can it? I would have never...you let me blab about it to the whole bar. You never said a thing. I mean, if any of that crazy monster stuff was true...I mean, come on. Just the part about sailing on a black ops ship into North Korean territory alone would make that whole thing highly classified."

"Yeah," I said, "I suppose so."

"Wish you hadn't told me that shit," Danny said, dragging a shaky hand across his brow. "Listen, we gotta go back in there and start spinning that shit. I mean, all of them drunks think you're a liar or nut anyway so just a final push. Could pass it all off as a joke."

He slapped me on the shoulder. Drinking buds. "Yeah," I said. "A joke. Yeah, it's a joke. Cosmic joke."

"Don't get morose on me, Iceman," he said, chuckling, dragging me back to the smoke-filled bar.

Danny started in with the joke plan, but once we were elbow deep into the next round, he changed his tact. "That's right, you barflies, this here motherfucker, my friend, the Iceman killed a real life Godzilla. Even has a bit of it in his stomach, just like he said."

I tried to quash his boasting. “Shhh….shh…” But by then, I was laughing too, and hanging onto the edge of the bar for dear life.

That’s when we noticed the two standing by the door.

“Sorry,” I said, “guess I should not have been so loose-lipped about the...you know.”

They were big men, older men, clean shaven and well dressed. They were important men. Military men, normally star-shouldered and decorated to their belly-buttons men, dressed in their version of incognito to meet with me about things no one should know about because none of it should be real.

“What can you tell me about your friend, Yoo Se Kwon?” the taller of the two asked.

“What can...I...not much…”

We were at a small back table that wobbled if you put your elbows on its surface.

“His death aboard the *Felicity* came at a very unfortunate time,” the other said. He was thick and round headed, his neck seeming to sprout out of the nice suit he wore beneath his coat. “The thing has collected all the remaining parts. Yuz had a crew. They had all taken pieces. They are all dead. Some were in Korea, some Japan. Three were here in the States.”

“Dead?” I asked. “How? Was it the Blue? Were they all taking it? I mean, it had to be what killed Yuz, and I suppose I’m next.”

“We think not,” the tall one said. “Se Kwon’s self-administered, self-monitored use of Prussian Blue was not very precise, to say the least. There had been rumors that the Bulgasari, while in re-acquisition mode, largely kept to the sea in order to get about. It is the team’s conclusion that Kwon was unable to follow the same precise dosage regimen aboard the fishing boats he had chartered. He likely passed the threshold into lethal toxicity even before you met him. At the Naval hospital you were closely monitored, the Blue titrated with great care. We’re not here to check on your medical status.”

I had nothing to say to this, only offering a shrug. *What then?*

The taller one continued, “I’ve read the transcript of your debriefing several times. I’m particularly interested in the smaller ones, the little monsters. What do you think they were?”

They had placed a bottle of water and coffee in front of me. I wanted to tell them I was better off with a beer. It was too late into the night to turn my drunk ship around.

“Do you know the difference between a dragon and a dinosaur?” I asked.

I could see them straighten, grit their teeth. They wanted to yell in my face, shake me; I could tell. It was a big thing to hunt monsters. Yuz and Lyons taught me that. And these two thought I had turned into a worthless drunk, a drunk that was jerking them around.

Their eyes said it. The wrong guy had lived, just a lowly ensign of little note.

“You’re all we got, Ensign Pinto,” the tall one said. I think of him as the General. “It’s made land and on the move.”

The other one, the thick-necked one, I thought of as the Admiral, cleared his throat. “In a way, we’re lucky,” he said. “North Korea is about as locked down as you can get. It operates in the shadows and hides, with great success, behind the parallel. We’ve been tracking the thing by satellite. It’s bigger than ever.”

“The Koreans have reached out to us,” the General said. “We have a plan. From what we can discern from your debrief and some of the notes Kwon made available to the project, we believe we can be successful.”

I took a slug of the water. “The difference between a dinosaur and a dragon is that a dino dies,” I said. “A dragon can do just about anything it wants, including forming smaller versions of itself out of whatever chunks we blow it to. Each chunk is a monster, fully capable of defending itself.”

“That’s what we thought too,” the Admiral said.

The General reached across the shaky table with a long hand. “Son,” he said, “we need to bring you in.”

“In? Into what?” I asked. “I don’t know anything.”

"You're not safe out here," the Admiral said. "We know you're still holding onto a section of the thing. It won't rest until it has it. As far as we can figure, the last one holding onto some of the flesh was another survivor of Il's movie production. Apparently, they had blown a piece off during the fighting. That man was working as a long distance trucker out of Okinawa. He was murdered three days ago, his stomach torn open, the contents spilled out. No monster bits about. But he was taking infusions of Prussian Blue."

"But the Blue isn't what killed him," I said.

The General shook his head. "No," he said. "Not the Blue."

I stood. I was sobering up and not happy about it.

"You guys successfully killed a drunk won by virtue of steadfast binge drinking," I said. "Look, I appreciate the spot you guys are in. I do. This is all a mystery, my friends. Dragons are creatures wrapped in mystery. Dinosaurs lived and dragons never die. Sorry dudes, or is it sirs? Excuse the informality and all, but I'm just Gary Pinto of Cherry Hill, New Jersey, and I got into the Navy because I loved my grandpa, pee-paw as I called him. Around here they know him as The Torpedo."

The Admiral smiled. "I'm well aware of the acts of the apostle Pinto," he said. "I have to wonder what he'd want you to do in this situation."

"I'll have to ask him when I see 'im," I said, taking a step toward the door.

The big older men pushed back from the table, their hair paired Q-tips of iron. "In exactly five days," said the General, "a team will be choppering into a landing site on Mount Paektu, tallest mountain in North Korea, a place sacred to the Party and ancient Korean religions alike. It's where the blacksmith of the ancient myth supposedly had gone to pray for the Bulgasari to rise and take up his cause somewhere around the time of the Trojan War. It's currently in the path the creature is taking. The North has successfully evacuated the regions between."

"Communists," the other snorted. "Efficient as hell, if nothing else."

"On the sixth day," said the General, "it will be discovered that the Koreans have recommenced nuclear testing. It will be further discovered that the detonation was so disastrous it will likely set their program back by a decade."

"That's convenient," I said.

"It's the trade off," the Admiral said.

The General nodded. "Un and his crew have guaranteed a ten-year moratorium."

I licked my thick lips. "In exchange for?"

"Our bomb," the Admiral said. "We will use the B61-12 super missile on the creature."

"An experimental device," the General added. "We've been working on it since we confirmed the existence of this thing. Implosion is the idea. Like napalm, but on a nuclear level. It'll blow the hell out of the area and then suck all the atmosphere off that mountain."

"Or, rather, set fire to the air itself," the Admiral corrected. "If the explosion, as powerful as anything ever tested, doesn't do the job, nothing living will breathe on that mountain for a month."

"Sounds like you got it worked out," I said, putting a hand on the rattly door. "I'm sure you know that if you fail, this thing will become unstoppable; it eats the radiation, makes it bigger and stronger. So, good luck, fellas."

"Ensign Pinto," the Admiral said, his tone pulling rank. "We need you. We need you in the clean-up team. To make sure the thing is done, for good."

I laughed. "Just go in and look around for pieces that looks like bait for mako sharks."

"It's not what we can see. That much we know," the General said. "There are other reasons why you'd have an inside track."

"I don't know what you are talking about." But I sorta did. "I'll give The Torpedo your love."

I stumbled out the door to the street. When I heard them calling after me, I ran.

A voice called after me, "The only treatment for survivor's guilt is doing good works!"

Spring had backed off its original promise of warmth. I stumbled through narrow streets in a general downward direction; our hero, The Iceman, hugged his jacket around him, making no particular headway toward home, the house owned by his parents. I am he, the hero of the story.

Sounds bounced weirdly between structures lining chipped concrete sidewalks where cars cluttered both sides so that the passage of other cars seemed unlikely in the choked arterial. Down a row of cars someone else climbed the slight incline, weaving toward me. I weaved too, trying to gauge the stranger's passage to give him room. Now I lost him. I leaned back toward the sidewalk but could not see him.

"Fuck 'em."

I continued down, down, down. The sound of something scuffling along the sidewalk made me stop.

"Hello?"

No reply. A map of the neighborhood I had grown up in formed in my mind. It was a good hike back to the street of my childhood. A more serious compass woke in me. Spinning on a heel, I started up the clogged street, the dark macadam glistening with an icy dew.

More subtle scuffles. The neighborhood of brick duplexes and steep concrete steps cupped sounds, letting them roll around.

"There's a bar full of soldiers right around the corner that know me."

Not sure what I tried to gain from that, particularly since the 'soldiers' I was referring to were deeper in the hole than one Gary Pinto. The monster meat in my stomach squirmed as though in answer to the movements of the figure.

"Fuck this."

I got my moxie on and got serious about finding my boyhood bed. There it was again, the shuffling sound, but impossible to tell from where--up ahead it seemed like. I plodded up the narrow street. A few parked vehicles ahead, a figure--only a few yards away--ducked behind a minivan. Hunched low, it looked like it was dressed much like the mystery officers who visited me at the VFW. The idea of those two older gents, who likely gave up on me and loaded themselves into a town car, stalking me like fanboys, made me smirk. While that was a silly image, someone *was* screwing with me, closing in.

Craning my neck every which way, I hunched over to peer under the van to see if I could confirm my new fan's whereabouts.

"Damn," I whispered and, once again, turned from the mystery figure. I had the feeling I was being corralled.

Considerably more sober, my heart starting to double time against my lungs, I whipped around and considered abandoning all dignity and breaking into a full run. Spinning, I faced something that froze me in my tracks. Peering through the door windows of a huge SUV, hungry eyes glared at me. The quick, short gasp I took in stung my lungs with morning chill.

I knew the face locked on me. The last time I confronted this face it was lodged on the slim, serpentine shoulders of the midget wrestler Bulgasari that gutted Lyons to take the last of the creature nuggets.

But the squirm in my guts reminded me this was not true. I had the last nugget.

My abdomen distended as the monster meat inside me responded to the thing crouching behind the SUV, yearning to return to this man-sized thing, sent out like a drone to retrieve the last part of itself so that it could be at full power, giant and omnipotent.

It was in that moment that I realized exactly what the shadow military brass wanted from me. The Iceman had become a Bulgasari early warning system.

A scream bounced around the concrete bowl of the narrow block, dripping wet with the pre-morning dew. I backed up into the sound of the scream I realized originated from me. The

SUV, black and oily, returned my scream as the man-sized Bulgasari (man-ga-sari, one might say) straightened to its full height, just short of seven feet, and let a claw slip absently down onto the hood of the big vehicle.

Why aren't you running? I asked my feet.

It hissed at me, a sound more sullenly victorious than aggressive.

"Leave me alone!" I bellowed. Running would have been better. It stepped out onto the street, the streetlight throwing strange shadows so that the thing's unusual spine formations changed and undulated, mimicking a general shape, which could pass as clothing.

The thing in me wriggled, with no small amount of glee, I thought.

My feet continued to fail to listen to my brain and I wondered, briefly, if those black marble eyes could hypnotize. A front door slammed down the block, perhaps the owner of the SUV coming to check the alarm.

"Hey," someone called. "Get away from my car."

It did not turn, only taking another step toward me. But I turned, and I ran. Up, down, wherever, don't know, just ran.

A storm of sounds fired up behind me as I was sure I was being pursued.

"You!" The unseen SUV man yelled at someone, not me, not my direction. "Don't come back here. I'll call the cops!"

The developed neighborhoods petered out pretty quickly, and I was running past blocks of swamp reeds and empty lots. The sound of my feet slapping the road died in the cool air. A dull blue rebounded off the clouds as the arriving sun distributed its cold radiance over the uncaring sky.

Then my dull foot thumps were answered by the hiss of something cutting through the reeds, something that wanted to stay off the road, stay hidden. My specialty diet of alcohol and shame was catching up with me. As afraid as I was, my legs threatened to leave me. My breath scraped through me in ragged wheezes. I wasn't going to make it. I swore I heard the thing in the weeds fly past me, to cut me off, but I dared not run back, let it box me in. I plunged on.

Up ahead, a derelict yellow construction vehicle sat in an empty lot, the back end of it, its rusted crane, leering over the right side of the road. I loped over to the left side to give myself room to react if (when) the monster leapt out from behind the cover of the truck.

My legs shook to a stop as I began to limp around the giant vehicle, sure death waited for me just beyond, but like a worn out game animal, I had no more to give.

A low growl issued from the opaque shadow the truck cast over the rest of the lot where it canceled the light from the sickly glow of the sodium arc lamp mounted on a tarred-up pole. I peered into the black, squinting and wiping at salty beads of sweat from my brow. My chest ached as I heaved for air. I may have let some of the beer out by peeing my pants. It was hard to tell with the flop sweat soaking through my cold spring layers.

The growling intensified. I could make out some movement, something low to the ground and furry. A dog. A big dog. Then I could make out other trucks and a metal shed next to a construction trailer. It wasn't just an empty lot. There was a fence in the back and a guard dog chained outside, and it was not growling at me. Something lurked in the deeper shadows of the lot.

The nervous dog barked and sprang at something blacker than the shadows. There was a scuffle.

I got myself going, hoping the dog would buy me time.

Growing up, I watched a lot of TV. New Jersey television content is funny. Between the New York and Philadelphia markets, New Jersey had a wealth of TV options, even in the pre-cable era. None so strange as local stations, some broadcasting in the dark web of TV land, UHF. One particular regularly scheduled cast of oddities sometimes included a strongman named Ulysses. A poorly groomed behemoth, Ulysses (not his birth name) would perform any number of odd but impressive strongman feats. One of them was taking a rubber hot water bottle and blowing it up, sorta like a balloon, except he did not stop at simply getting it inflated. Nope. He would blow and blow, Ulysses' mighty intercostal muscles against a pound of rubber poured into the shape of a huge, artificial bladder. And don't you know it, Ulysses won that battle, man versus rubber, every time. Every time. Boy, didn't he look proud, Ulysses, all red-cheeked beneath his brushfire of a beard. So proud.

I ran. Wasn't even wearing shoes good for running. Hadn't run that much since basic, but now recovering from, not just a drunk, but a series of drunks that had so wasted my traumatized body away, my heart threatened to burst. Burst, like some great, unseen giant grabbed me by my neck and extruded into me powerful gusts of awful atmosphere, shot forth by forces as yet not understood in their power, inscrutable and inescapable in their intent to rip me open like a birthday balloon in the hands of an inattentive seven-year-old, a hot water bottle witnessed on grainy UHF waves, floating unseen into the mind of young Gary Pinto.

Oh yeah, I ran. Without hope, I ran, puny legs of a puny man, running from a monster older than mountains. Behind me somewhere, in cold pursuit no doubt, a creature with long, tireless legs and powerful dragon lungs that blew fear into the hearts of its enemies shadowed me. There was no getting away, but I ran, blind and directionless, fleeing in mad panic.

The marshland surrounding the big ponds gave way to other buildings, some industrial like where the Bulgasari faced off against the big dog. Then a series of medical buildings.

"Oh geez, oh geez," I had been gasping, probably for some time. When I saw one towering building, burning bright with lights like the medical buildings, I stopped. I was among workers, in equal parts nursing outfits as laypersons, and some old folks, really old folks. Just a few of them, coming out into the new morning, bent so low they looked like they could tie their shoes without sitting down.

East Meadows, it read in huge red lettering on the side of the building. I knew the name.

My grandfather lived inside, on the fifth floor. My father wanted him somewhere close enough to visit. He had lived with us until my parents had gotten too old themselves to care for him as dementia dragged him into a twilight world of flat-lined routines and universal strangeness. Grandpa Morris, The Torpedo, lived up there, on the fifth floor, and he would not remember who I am. Maybe that was okay. Maybe that was fine. I went inside, limping a bit, wheezing a lot.

I signed in. I guess they knew who I was. Was not even sure it was visiting hours yet, and I looked a mess. They knew who I came to see. The Torpedo was not bound to be fussy.

I knew the room number. He had lived in East Meadows a while, at least since the beginning of my tour in the Pacific.

A floor nurse was leaving as I entered the room. "We got him up for you," she said at the door. "Got him dressed and cleaned up. Want him looking good for the family, looking good for the regular Thursday visit."

Thursday? Somewhere out there, the Bulgasari approached, as did my parents. Gramps got gussied for them, not for me.

"Thanks," I muttered, wondering about my appearance, about how I smelled. The nurse did not seem to notice.

He was a small figure, shrunken in his wheelchair, his back to me.

I let a gentle hand sweep over one sweater-clad shoulder. "Hey, Pee-paw," I said, taking the armchair that had been situated opposite the old man. "How's the road? How fast can you get that thing up to?"

His eyes rolled in my direction. "Uh," he grunted.

The Torpedo had been a big man once, in both physical and reputational stature. Lord knows his shadow still hung over me. Military-wise, the specter of The Torpedo kept a lot of the lights green on my career path. Since dad didn't go military, I was something of a proxy for Gramps. Around Cherry Hill, they called me Iceman and didn't mean it as a joke. My moniker seemed a sensible link to the grandeur of The Torpedo. Now Morris Hannon Pinto sagged low into his wheelchair, the once broad shoulders shrunk down to bony bookends at either side of the lolling head.

Outside, a commotion of some kind sent the sound of loud voices climbing up the side of the building from the parking lot and the abandoned lot that separated the retirement tower from the next medical facility down the road.

I jumped up from my chair to look down where the new day lit up the surrounding area.

Down below, an orderly was flipping off an ambulance driver that almost took out the old man the orderly escorted out to a walking path that surrounded the facility. The pussy willow trees lining the walkway were budding. A dark figure slipped between some of the thicker assembly of trees. I pulled away from the window, heart pounding.

"I thought this might be safe," I said to Pee-Paw. "Not even sure how I got here, just ran. But once I saw where I was, I thought that with the people around, it wouldn't dare try to slip into this place. It's a fish out of water, so to speak. Probably swam up the Delaware, sectioned off this bit of itself to come and get the last of the pieces we took. That thing out there, in dim light, it looks like someone moving in the shadows, makes those back spines it has look like an oversized coat. I dunno. I don't think it will chance being exposed."

"Uh," The Torpedo grunted, his filmy eyes finding me then losing me. At least he wasn't drooling. His last round of medications made him drool. "Da...the…"

"It must really need this last chunk. Maybe it's a matter of pride for this thing," I said, peeling back the blinds a couple of inches to peek down at the trees. "Can a monster be prideful? A dragon isn't a lizard, you know. We're not dealing with a lost dinosaur here, Gramps. Who knows how a legendary creature, something out of myth, like a minor god or something...who knows how it thinks? But one thing's for sure--"

"...first st...steps to Heaven…"

Words died in my mouth. "Wha…" Was this some kind of sick set up? "What did you say, Pee-Paw?"

Whatever it was, he had a heck of a time spitting it out while keeping his lower plate in his mouth. "Second tenet...second...to Heaven… is...contemplate the unknowable..."

"Are you shitting me?"

I left the room seeking answers from someone with a few more brain cells firing. I found an attendant wandering back and forth from rooms, delivering neatly folded linens.

"Excuse me," I said to him. "Do you know my grandfather, Morris H. Pinto? He's just down the hall there."

The attendant stopped and followed the direction of my finger through thick-lensed glasses, smiling. "Oh, The Torpedo, huh?" he said, a rakish glint behind the deeply refracting lenses. "Of course, we're all big fans of your grandfather here. He's a real hoot, or, at least, was when he first got here. Had more good days than bad back then."

"Could you tell me who's been to visit him? He just said something alarming...strange to me, and I wondered where he picked it up."

"What was it he said?"

"Did he ever say anything to you, or did you hear him mention something about the pathway to Heaven?"

The attendant seemed to think this over while he dumped out some used towels, removed his vinyl gloves and gathered up a fresh pile of terrycloth. "That sounds like some of that Korean stuff your grandfather talks about. Particularly with your dad. They're both hot on that stuff. I guess The Torpedo was stationed out there."

Well, it was hard to measure my level of shock, but I shook myself clear and nodded. "Yeah," I said. "That's why I wanted to be stationed in that theater, and my dad was an Asian studies major at Rutgers. I'm glad they had something to talk about."

"It was good to see on those good days."

I peered around the corner, caught a glimpse of those sharp shoulders beneath the soft sweater. "Still," I said, "that's an odd one to hook onto, don't ya think? I mean, what is Korean Heaven, anyway?"

The attendant wrestled on a new pair of gloves. "Yeah, well, that's one they went on about as those good days ran out," he said. "From what I could catch, the Path to Heaven is an obscure Christian sect that made its home on the Peninsula. This group was, is--whatever--big into pilgrimages, particularly to this one mountain, biggest one in North Korea."

"Mount Paektu," I said.

"Yeah, yeah, I think that's the one."

I looked back and forth from the depleted Torpedo to the attendant with the big glasses. There was an insistent buzzing sound and something bit into my left thigh. Leaping and screaming, I made the attendant jump, his mouth dropping to a shocked *O* and the new towels were sent flying in a crazed flutter of pastel cloth.

I grabbed for my leg to fend off some inch high version of the Bulgasari that had made its way into the rest home to gnaw at me. "Oh," I said, adrenaline washing out of me. "Oh. It's uh...my phone. I forgot I had it. Half the time I leave it at the VFW hall."

There was a text from my father.

"Thanks," I said to the attendant. "And, sorry for the scare."

He nodded, eyeing me with a good degree less trust through the coke bottle specs. He continued down the hallway with his cart of cloth.

Going to see Pee-Paw. You should come along. It read.

Not much concern about where I had been all night. But that wasn't much of a mystery. Waking up at Dan's place happened most mornings.

Already there, I returned.

Great! We'll be there in a few.

"You know the difference between a dragon and dinosaur?" I asked the attendant who was already gone when I looked up. I talked down into the phone instead. "A dragon has a destiny."

Dad, I wrote, *I gotta call for a ride from a couple of DANICO big wigs. It's time I got back to work.*

It was knocking on my door for some time, and I didn't have it in me to shut my eyes to it anymore.

"Dragons are all about destiny," I said to the empty hallway. Out of a room to my right a quavering voice called for his slippers. "And I guess I am too."

I punched in the number for the monster hunters. I hoped the General and the Admiral had big smiles on their faces when I saw them next. I knew the smaller, man-sized thing outside would be happy too. It could head back to Korea. I was bringing the last bit of Bulgasari back to its home.

THIRTEEN

Who knows what the Bulgasari had been up to in the North Korean countryside, but the North was more than happy to welcome the DANICO secret mission into their midst. The chopper looked like it was built during the Korean War. It was open, and the ride was cold.

Below, the bare expanse that was the most northern regions of the Korean peninsula passed in austere, cryogenic sadness. It was a land short on means and long on threadbare mythology.

I tried to call to the Koreans manning the craft; a pilot, a copilot, and a Party official as escort. "This mountain, Paektu, it must be awfully important?"

No answer.

No doubt the unfiltered sound of the rotors kept them from hearing me. "Why is it going there, do you think? What does it want at that place?" I screamed into the frigid thrum of the blades, pulling my hand inside the sleeves of the parka issued to me.

There was a tap at the helmet the Party official had slammed onto my noggin. Next to me on the long, barely cushioned bench sat Brady Plummet, the DANICO leader I had been referring to as the Admiral. At least I had gotten the Navy part right, I learned.

He smiled at me and pulled down the microphone lodged onto the helmet by way of a retracting arm. Puffs of steam preceded speech from his mouth. "They won't talk to you," he said. "Do you know why North Korean Airlines has the worst safety rating worldwide?"

The Party official eyed Plummet, the Admiral, but said nothing, going back to examining the harsh land below.

"Doesn't seem to be the most lavish land," I said, still having to shout a bit. "I can't imagine they have the most up-to-date or well-maintained equipment."

The Admiral, who, in reality, never rose above the rank of RDML-07, lower rear admiral (let loose the butt jokes), shook his head. “The reason they have the highest crash rate is because of pilot error which, normally, would be caught by the back-up, the co-pilot; however, North Korean pilots have a higher Party ranking than their cabin mate. The co-pilot is trained to let the plane crash rather than correct a Party superior.”

The Party official glanced at us. Did I catch a slim smile on his face?

“So these guys are not going to chat with you, Gary,” he said. “They got orders. But to give you context, I’ll offer some information about where we are going, and maybe it has to do with the path the Bulgasari is taking--who knows. Paektu Mountain is central to the regional mythology, even for the Chinese, who border the north side of the mountain. All you have to do is take a peek at the North Korean national logo to see its importance.”

He turned and tapped a square at the back of his Korean military issue helmet. Beneath a pulsing red star dribbling red rays down over the other figures on the patch, stood a series of mountains--rendered in rigorous lines--in which the central mountain stood above the rest like the chief goose pimple on the arm of a child who lost the snowball fight.

“It’s where the Kim family, according to Party myth, draws its rightful sovereignty. Being a powerful image of might and all, both Il and Un are the latest of the Peaktu bloodline,” Plummet said. “Going back to roughly what would be the medieval period for these folks, the great general called upon Tangun to send forth a demon to help conquer the overwhelming forces of his foes and got instead the Bulgasari, a very pissed off monster, summoned by a pissed off dad of a daughter the general had raped. But, too, the crater at the top of the mountain, a barely dormant volcano, holds what some of the mystic Christian sects refer to as Heaven Lake. Your buddy, Se Kwon? He was a follower of Lee Yusin, the leader of a cult-like group called Wonsan Sinhaksan.”

The North Koreans in the chopper laughed and repeated the name of the sect in mock triumphant tones.

“First landmark, huh?” the Party man said in mangled English that was hard to make out. “Path a Heaven, huh?”

The communists laughed.

Godless communists, The Torpedo would say, perhaps spitting on the ground as final punctuation. Maybe that was the biggest threat to the Red Dynasty in this scenario. A God was coming, an ancient God of ancient times that are no more, a timeless thing to remind the Peaktu bloodline that they too are but temporary and that the Kim Jung Uns of the world, on a grand scale, are as good as gone, the dinosaurs of the geopolitical landscape.

My guts wriggled.

"There," Plummet said, pointing out the front, between the pilots, where a series of peaks rose up out of the earth before us. They were all monsters, but the closest were lowly acolytes, serving the giant at the end of the canyon of mountains, a pile of rock whose icy top melded with the lowering gray of the sky.

"So," I said, "bottom line, why is it going up there? Why that mountain?"

Plummet indicated something tucked under the bench the Party member sat upon. The North Korean passed it over. It was a device I had become familiar with.

The Admiral unhooked a wand from the box and, after flipping a switch or two, passed it over the part of my parka that covered my abdomen. The box made some clicking sounds, nothing too alarming. The needle on the dials jumped a bit. He took the wand and turned it back on his own middle. Nothing.

"We're not sure how Se Kwon figured it out, but Prussian Blue does have a dampening effect on free radicals coming off radioactive materials," he said. "Peaktu Mountain was the site of one of the first missile tests performed by the new regime. There was grave concern worldwide--the Chinese in particular--that the premier test of the Korean's Bright Star program, a maximum payload ballistic missile, would set off the sleeping volcano that is Mount Peaktu. The North Koreans have a long history of accidents during these tests."

"And was there, an accident?"

He nodded. "It's what woke this thing up, we're sure of it," he said. "Peaktu did not erupt but it cracked open a bit, just enough to allow the radioactive fallout from the detonation to leak down into the earth. None of us can pretend to know what that thing is, what Yoo Se Kwon thought of as the Bulgasari, that ancient Korean mythical creature. How it functions, particularly how it metabolizes certain free ions, who knows. Thanks to you, we have two well-preserved bodies...specimens, but not much has come of examining Lyons and Yuz yet. Stick to the facts, I say: It is here. We have the record of what Se Kwon encountered during the making of the infamously bad movie, *Pulgasari*, but--"

"You mean there actually is a movie?"

Plummet chuckled. "Yeah," he said. "Not worth watching but the dad, Il, did complete that movie, and it does have a few seconds of what we believe is actual footage of the creature, likely from the day it tore up the camp and was buried back in the earth. Those sequences are actually quite brutal."

The Korean pilots started spouting in Korean and pointing toward the ground. I turned to peer down at the passing landscape, the brutal, barren landscape. A figure moved among a frail looking stand of fir trees, towering above them but still just the largest dot among other dots passing below us. It moved, from my vantage, the way a large ice floe moves on a frozen lake that's considering thawing out, slow but powerfully, inexorably charging on a landscape of other, geologic giants, heading back home. The thing in my stomach migrated so that it pressed against my belly button in response to the proximity to the giant below.

Korean pilot spoke some more. We had dipped a bit starboard to get a look at the giant serpent wending its way higher and higher into the mountains. Now he straightened the chopper.

"We'll be there in about a half hour," Plummet said.

We used a launch pad for the failed Bright Star-1 as our landing site. The air smelled of burning tires. We cleared the summit, a vicious, northern wind buffeting the aircraft. My nerves on edge, I grappled for support among a wallow of unused seatbelts. The thing in my stomach danced with glee. It was going home, quicker if the chopper crashed.

But it didn't crash. We circled and spun and came down dead-center on a launch pad that was now a landing pad.

No sooner was I on the ground, the chopper blades thrusting me toward the downward, than I thought I felt slight tremors shake my feet. I shook my head. The Bulgasari was too far away for that. *Wasn't it?*

Plummet grabbed me by the elbow. "Come look," he said. I pulled down my ski cap over my ears and followed. The edge of the landing pad looked down over Heaven Lake. The beams of the powerful mounted lights surrounding the crater sunk into cloudy depths, setting the lake aglow, white rays penetrating into the icy water too deep to allow the beams to find bottom. The water was blue, Prussian Blue.

"That's where you're luring it to?" I asked. "I thought you had your doubts about said Prussian pigment?"

The Admiral shrugged. "For all we know that's where the thing is going anyway," he said. "And it turns out, after some deeper research, that Prussian Blue is highly effective against cesium poisoning as well as thallium. Cesium is a radioactive isotope."

"You mean that a professor of geology might have known some rarer qualities of a mineral?" I said, hoping I sounded more playful than sarcastic. Plummet was my ride home. "Imagine that."

He smiled. "We pumped it into the lake. We're about to double down on the creature's radioactivity. Maybe there's a wavelength that will kill it, or the sheer blast will blow it to bits and when it falls into the Blue...well, we have hopes. Plus, whatever other metabolic oddities makes this thing go, we do know it breathes. Satellite data shows it is an oxygen-based organism, aerobic metabolism, and that missile targeting this mountain top has a warhead equipped with a device that will burn off all the oxygen from this area for at least a week. We predict a firestorm that can be seen from space."

"Will it work?"

He shrugged. "Our job, your job really, is to hold it here, in case it wasn't actually planning on making this its summer home."

"How am I..?" But I knew. "The piece inside me. It will try to take it."

"Seems like it will, predictably, go out of its way to reacquire it."

Peering down into the glowing blue water, I sighed. I knew my role. I looked at the Admiral and nodded. It made sense. The final sacrifice.

The thudding never stopped and now it was obvious and insistent.

Yeah, it did not take a genius to figure the score. Even a lowly ensign could see the writing on the bulkhead. I was destined for the lake, a final cumshaw, a fuck-you-very-much for your service.

I mean, really, I got it. This missile thing had to work. It had to. If it lived, the Koreans would not keep to the deal, the moratorium. That meant more nuclear testing, more loose radiation for the Bulgasari to suck up like pasta. The thing would probably just get bigger, a reptilian planet of its own, a bi-pedal Mount Olympus (Peaktu) striding the Earth in great bounds, crushing as it goes, a living tectonic movement. A dragon quake would rock the world, even little Cherry Hill, New Jersey. It was the least I could do to keep the home fires burning. I never talked about this whole adventure with my parents. It could be they knew. I certainly didn't keep any secrets from my VFW buds. At least my friends at DANICO would know that I saved the world.

"This last little part of the Bulgasari," I said, "you were right, and you were wrong. It seems like you thought I was special. I'm not, what is inside me is. I thought it was special, like maybe a chunk of its amygdala or prostate or something. I wasn't sure how much you knew."

"Figures."

I glared at him quizzically.

The thunderous tread of the creature rattled through us. The thing's little self pranced within me. A growl like a fifty ton, steel crane made to genuflect under the weight of a Croniun hand. A frigid wind took hold of the monstrous cry and swirled it around the peak so that it dipped into the crater lake, bounced around the bowl so that it seemed that the mountain itself screamed, the crater an open mouth drowning in Prussian Blue.

"Yuz, as you call him, had folks all over with chunks of that thing inside them," Plummet shouted over the thuds and screaming wind. He lifted a walkie talkie and blurted a few words into it I could not hear. "That thing tracked them all down, even to Frisco."

I nodded and edged toward the precipice dropping down into the lake. I got the tip of my shoe over the edge and heard Plummet gasp. I turned to see a cobra head the size of a tugboat crest the jagged ridge of the crater, the snoring mouth of the sleeping volcano. Through the swirling spume of dust and detritus in the light of a sun playing hide-and-seek with the remains of the day.

"It's time," I said and edged forward. "Gotta get in the crater, right? Gotta hold it here."

I said a shaky prayer and leaned out. A vice grip at my shoulder stopped me from going over.

"What the hell you doing?" Plummet asked, his eyes wide.

I looked at him, confused. The monster got a taloned paw on the edge of the crater like a swimmer grabbing the pool ledge to hoist himself up.

"Have to get the piece of it into the crater," I said. "Gotta keep it here so that the missile can do its work."

He continued to eye me strangely while he removed a glove and reached into a pouch in his parka. He brought out a vial. "We were thinking of this," he said, holding the tube out in front of me. "It's a mimetic."

"Up-chuck juice."

It washed over me, and if the lighting were better here at the hellish environs of Heaven Lake, he may have seen me blush.

"Oh." I took the vial.

"Don't know what you were planning," he said, "but I was hoping on being a safe distance from here. Meanwhile, you were just about the only safe container for that thing. The radiation coming off the little bit of monster could light up the Rockefeller Christmas tree."

"So, I'm likely dead anyway."

He shrugged. "Who knows," he said. "Yuz seemed to have a better idea of the secret qualities of blue pigments."

I said nothing. But we both knew. Yuz was dead. But I liked the idea of seeing home after removing the monster from the world, and my life.

The creature lurched over the rim, dragging a great skyscraper of a leg over the rim, breaking loose jagged bits of rock, rolling down into the crater to splash into Heaven Lake.

I popped the top on the vial and swallowed the contents. In a moment I was at the edge losing every bit of my innards. Though the complimentary breakfast at the Korean military base's commissary launched down into the blue, and then what seemed like gallons of bilious spew, there was no monster bit inside. It was as if it refused to leave. I coughed and retched, trying to get it out of me. The empty vial tumbled from my hand.

The Bulgasari pulled itself to its full height, finding it hard to get purchase--its head well into the swirling clouds.

I coughed again, trying to get the bottom of my intestinal tract. The force of the cough caused a spasm in the region covered by my boxers.

"Oh no," I said, already loosening my belt. "Not from that end. Ugh."

The Admiral shrugged, trying to hide a grin.

I hesitate now, as I write this official debriefing report that, for sure, will never see the light of day, to offer up what happened next. Not many of the things I did during this time were acts to be proud of. And, I surely would not say I was proud of slipping my hand into my soiled skivvies, but they say in the final hour, at the moment that will decide who takes the day--humans or dragon gods--a soldier, a sailor has to dig deep inside to find the hero. Don't know if I found a hero in my nasty boxers, and what was inside was now outside, but I did it. It was nasty, but I did it.

I stood there with a handful of my processed dinner with a solid clump of monster in it. I turned toward the creature that looked down from the running clouds with disdainful, serpentine hate at the lowly beings that had, long ago, both called it forth from some unholy hollow within the Earth only to spend our time bedeviling it with something like buyer's remorse.

I half expected to see the Bulgasari staring down at me with the same disgust. The Admiral radiated at me from my left. The beast stepped toward us, to recover the last bit of itself and become whole. I gave the caked hand a shake and managed to send the fecal, steaming clump down into the blue lake.

"Good work, Ensign," Plummet said. I just looked at him with a sickened, sideways grin. "Come on, we've done our part. Need to hightail it out of here."

He grabbed me by the shoulder and pulled back toward the helicopter. I tried to shake the loose bits of crap from my hand.

"Think I need a towel," I said, not expecting a response. The triumphant growl of the beast eddied the angry swirl of the storm clouds.

Another helicopter carrying the Korean prep team was already up in the tumult, disappearing into the night. In the blue bowl, the Bulgasari waded into what appeared to be bottomless waters. Presumably reuniting with its final piece, it howled in triumph at the knotted clouds; the scene playing out in the banks of stadium lights the prep crew had erected.

"Get us up, now!" the Admiral barked into his helmet mic, giving a twirling signal with his hand. "Saint George, Saint George! This is Beanstalk, let Slingshot fly. Repeat, let Slingshot fly!"

I fought to get strapped in with one hand still caked in my own shit. The chopper lifted precariously off the landing pad, one side canting heavily to the side. The pilot shouted, maybe cursing the wind, maybe crying out for the ghost of Kim Jung Il to save him. He straightened us and we were aloft.

We'd have a way to go to get above the weather, and all the while, we only succeeded--in unsteady progress--to bring ourselves face-to-face with the Bulgasari. Distracted by the movement of the chopper, the creature stepped to the edge of the crater, tracking us with its eyes.

"It's going to leave," I yelled. "We failed."

Perched on the edge of the crater, teetering on slipping off the mountain summit, the Bulgasari sniffed the air, sometimes appearing to want to give us chase, sometimes distracted by something in the crater.

"No," Plummet returned. "It hasn't left the lake, ground zero for the missile. It must still be looking for its lost part. Maybe it doesn't want to touch it given the condition it's in, let it soak for a while."

He was laughing at me. The Bulgasari lost its grip on the crater lip, its great mass dragging it down into the lake. It reached for us with desperate strikes of the vicious claws, but unwilling to move its legs from the lake.

The pilot yelled some more, his copilot looking rather sheepish as his leader cursed the wind.

The furious claws almost got us, each talon the size of one of the helicopter blades. The pilot cursed again and banked us severely to the starboard, a keenly-sharpened claw just missing us.

Up and up, until we pierced the heart of the clouds to get a glance at the last of the daylight, a distant, receding glow. Below, the Bulgasari bellowed in rage. In the deepening blue of the night sky, a first, unvanquishable star, or planet, burned bright at the eastern horizon.

Plummet corrected me on this assessment. "Slingshot," he barked into his com, "the missile."

It was coming fast. Swerving, but with great speed, we escaped the old volcano and the wreath of clouds strangling it. The stadium lights were visible through the brackish swirl, casting a writhing silhouette of some hideous thing contained within the cloud funnel, a giant thing, swaying in slow cobra movements, howling back at the storm. Then the lights went out, and we were nearly out of sight of Peaktu. I swear I could hear the cries of the beast over the *womp* of chopper blades and through my airman helmet.

"Come on! We got to be another five klicks in about one minute!" Plummet yelled at no one in particular, the receding storm maybe.

The pilot yelled in Korean too, probably echoing the Admiral's concerns. I don't know how far we were when the missile hit, but the entire sky lit as though someone was turning on bright, overhead lights on a group that had been sitting in the dark for hours.

There was an initial blast wave that first pushed us away from Peaktu, then a great sucking that ripped us back. We all screamed. I hung onto cargo straps with my crappy hand and screamed. The air got thin quickly as though someone had opened a door in outer space. My ears popped.

The pilot screamed and cursed. We were going down.

Suddenly, the helicopter cabin was spinning while the rotors seemed to stay still. Though we were all trained military, we all screamed. The pilot thrust the stick in several directions, finally pulling it into his gut. Hard to tell what the pilot was up to with all his communist cursing, but he slowed the spin so that the rotors were doing more of the work, slowing our fall down into the barren wasteland of North Korean mountains.

We pulled out of the spin and regained lift. Behind us, an orange glow suffused the mountain peaks, a new sun had risen, one without warmth. For a moment, orange ruled the world, for just a moment.

A nearly subsonic hum carried through the mountains as the clouds over Peaktu boiled over into the surrounding topography, punching the anaerobic landscape with bolts of lightning. We could see trees, small and pathetic, wither like daffodils under a tropical sun.

It had to be done. They had turned a spot on the Earth essentially into the surface of Mercury. Nothing could survive the new climate of Peaktu, let alone the solar storm the detonation had released.

Then a cracking sound tore through the chopper, a sound that deafened us right through the helmets. The artificial sunset at the top of the big mountain went from hot glow of vespers to the brutal fire of lunch in the Sahara. The world went red. Peaktu was erupting.

"Get us out of here!" the Admiral cried.

The pilot did not have to be told twice. He gunned it, the nose of the craft dipping with forward intent as the pilot tilted the big rotor wash behind us and sent us rocketing forward. Fireballs pasted the countryside. If the barren landscape appeared harsh before, it was a true hellscape now.

The chopper flew farther away, but Peaktu only burned brighter, seemingly lighting the whole continent before us. I wondered, briefly, how they—DANICO and the North Koreans--would explain this event. Would they let the North

Koreans take the hit: continuance of secret nuclear testing gone wrong? Would make some sense; they had the most to lose if the beast were left to roam. But they had something to offer in execution of the end game as well. Secrecy.

As impenetrable as time itself, current events shrouded in layers of isolation and disinformation so deep, puncturing the veil drawn along the 38th parallel becomes equivalent to an archeological dig. As far as the West was concerned, North Korea may as well operate in the Bronze Age. All that can be known is the bits of hard evidence to be reassembled into a pattern. A trail of evidence that deifies the slippery notion of sense as each find reveals a narrative spinning the yarn of living monsters and the wholesale destruction of a mountain achieved by reviving the sleeping volcano beneath. The artifacts exist, but you have to dig deep to learn the story of enemy nations coming together to stop an ancient creature from breaching the curtains of time to end the modern world.

The chopper flew on, as did time, as I survived the night of the volcano and was ejected out the ancient world of the Kim Jungs into the modern world of perpetual movement of knowledge, the unceasing climate of change.

I flew, island hopping across the Pacific before landing in the San Diego naval facility at Point Loma where I found myself, sometime later, almost settled back into the real world with a new, real position.

With no desire to return to the sea, nor the Far East, a genuine need for my experiences directed me toward Naval Intelligence Command. There, I became both subject and investigator in counter-intelligence, reacting directly to incidents of cesium poisoning, likely assassination attempts. We work regularly with Prussian Blue.

I became leader of a response team that would train others on signs of cesium poisoning and how to respond with the blue.

Now a full lieutenant (L-3), my end of the team was running late for a high-pressure briefing for a congresswoman and her delegation. We all had been downing Starbucks on our way to the southern base across town. My two male assistants accompanied me to the bathroom where I performed a familiar trick. Now more of a pale, glacial blue, the stream dropping out of me into the tall wall urinal invited comment.

"I knew it," said the one ensign, the one from Kentucky. "You been dipping into the Prussian stash."

The other laughed along. "Naw," replied the other ensign, a grade ahead and also from Jersey. "That's why they call him the Iceman, veins of Artic seawater."

I laughed. It was genuine. I had returned to service, and was happy to find my place.

The First Landmark on the Path to Heaven is radical acceptance.

We burst into the conference room. I tossed apologies in various directions around the long table with the congresswoman at the center position who had given up on us and was taking a phone call.

I apologized further, profusely even, but the congresswoman continued to talk on the phone as Lieutenant Junior Grade, Penny Martel (the one who could not join us in the bathroom) uploaded the PowerPoint she had so effectively compiled. Just as the first figures demonstrating number and region of cesium attacks appeared on the whiteboard at the end of the room opposite the congresswoman, the seemingly urgent call ceased, and we had the congresswoman's undivided attention, which did not make me feel particularly relaxed.

"Just a second," she said. "Don't I know you?"

I shrugged. "Don't think so, ma'am."

"Yes, I do," she said. "You're Gary Pinto, and you are at the center of one of my favorite conspiracy theories spouted by members of the other party. Wild stuff claiming there was a cover-up from the previous administration that the last round of nuclear treaty talks with North Korea broke down because of the Peaktu eruption which, according to these poor demented souls, was caused by one of our missiles. In this theory, we fired this missile in secret coordination with the North Korean government in order to take down, hah...ready for this...a giant creature that had escaped from below the surface of the Earth hungry to destroy humanity, the race that had enslaved it years before in the earth. I love that one! I swear these red-faced radio hosts have invented a whole new genre, conspiracy horror, monster espionage. I mean, come on, can you believe it?"

She owned the room, driving the laughter.

"Well, what can I tell you about monsters?" I said. "Not much really. I can tell you something a friend of mine shared with me while I was stationed in the Pacific Theater--probably why my name comes up in that story. He told me the First Landmark on the Path to Heaven is radical acceptance."

The congresswoman was still enjoying the incredulous laughter bubbling about the room, but let her eyes drift back to me.

"Wha—?" she asked.

"Some things just are," I said. "It's hard to believe that creatures the size of this building ever roamed our planet, but they did. You know the difference between a dragon and a dinosaur?"

She didn't seem all that interested in my question nor in the distinction, still laughing it up with her squad.

"The difference between the two is that dinosaurs are accepted as fact, and dragons don't care," I said. "Now, if I could have your attention…"

@severedpress
/severedpress

Check out other great

Sea Monster Novels!

Michael Cole

SCAR

Scar is a killing machine. Born from DNA spliced between the extinct Megalodon and modern day Great White, he has a viciousness that transcends time. His evil is reflected in his eyes, his savagery in his two-inch serrated teeth, his ruthlessness in his trail of death. After escaping captivity, the killer shark travels to the island community Cross Point, where prey is in abundance. With an insatiable appetite, heightened senses, and skin impervious to bullets, Scar kills everything that crosses his path. His reign of terror puts him at war with the island sheriff, Nick Piatt. With the body count rising, Nick vows to protect his island community from the vicious threat. With the aid of a marine biologist, a rookie deputy, and a bad-tempered fisherman, Nick leads a crusade against Scar, as well as the ruthless scientist who created him.

Rick Chesler

HOTEL MEGALODON

An underwater luxury hotel on a gorgeous tropical island is set for an extravagant opening weekend with the world watching. The only thing standing in the way of a first-rate experience for the jet-setting VIPs is an unscrupulous businessman and sixty feet of prehistoric shark. As the underwater complex is besieged by a marauding behemoth, newly minted marine biologist Coco Keahi must face off against the ancient predator as it rises from the deep with a vengeance. Meanwhile, a human monster has decided he would be better off if Coco were one of the creature's victims.

Check out other great

Sea Monster Novels!

Matt James

SUB-ZERO

The only thing colder than the Antarctic air is the icy chill of death... Off the coast of McMurdo Station, in the frigid waters of the Southern Ocean, a new species of Antarctic octopus is unintentionally discovered. Specialists aboard a state-of-the-art DARPA research vessel aim to apply the animal's "sub-zero venom" to one of their projects: An experimental painkiller designed for soldiers on the front lines. All is going according to plan until the ship is caught in an intense storm. The retrofitted tanker is rocked, and the onboard laboratory is destroyed. Amid the chaos, the lead scientist is infected by a strange virus while conducting the specimen's dissection. The scientist didn't die in the accident. He changed.

Alister Hodge

THE CAVERN

When a sink hole opens up near the Australian outback town of Pintalba, it uncovers a pristine cave system. Sam joins an expedition to explore the subterranean passages as paramedic support, hoping to remain unneeded at base camp. But, when one of the cavers is injured, he must overcome paralysing claustrophobia to dive pitch-black waters and squeeze through the bowels of the earth. Soon he will find there are fates worse than being buried alive, for in the abandoned mines and caves beneath Pintalba, there are ravenous teeth in the dark. As a savage predator targets the group with hideous ferocity, Sam and his friends must fight for their lives if they are ever to see the sun again.

@severedpress
/severedpress

Check out other great

Sea Monster Novels!

Michael Cole

CREATURE OF LAKE SHADOW

It was supposed to be a simple bank robbery. Quick. Clean. Efficient. It was none of those. With police searching for them across the state, a band of criminals hide out in a desolate cabin on the frozen shore of Lake Shadow. Isolated, shrouded in thick forest, and haunted by a mysterious history, they thought it was the perfect place to hide. Tensions mount as they hear strange noises outside. Slain animals are found in the snow. Before long, they realize something is watching them. Something hungry, violent, and not of this world. In their attempt to escape, they found the Creature of Lake Shadow.

C.J. Waller

PREDATOR X

When deep level oil fracking uncovers a vast subterranean sea, a crack team of cavers and scientists are sent down to investigate. Upon their arrival, they disappear without a trace. A second team, including sedimentologist Dr Megan Stoker, are ordered to seek out Alpha Team and report back their findings. But Alpha team are nowhere to be found – instead, they are faced with something unexpected in the depths. Something ancient. Something huge. Something dangerous. Predator X

www.ingramcontent.com/pod-product-compliance
Lightning Source LLC
Chambersburg PA
CBHW061241170626
46809CB00007B/2781

* 9 7 8 1 9 2 2 5 5 1 9 1 7 *